Black Mare Books

SPACE CITY 6

Additional Books by the Space City Scribes

Mandy Broughton
The Cat's Last Meow
Cream Cape and
the Case of the Missing Hamster

Artemis Greenleaf
Earthbound
The Hangman's Wife

Ellen Leventhal and Ellen Rothberg
Don't Eat the Bluebonnets
Hayfest – A Holiday Quest

K. C. Maguire
Dear John
Ivory Tower

Monica Shaughnessy
The Tell-Tail Heart
Doom & Gloom

SPACE CITY 6

Houston Stories from the Weird to the Wonderful

The Space City Scribes:
Mandy Broughton
Artemis Greenleaf
Ellen Leventhal
K. C. Maguire
Ellen Rothberg
Monica Shaughnessy

PUBLISHED BY:

Black Mare Books

Houston, Texas

www.blackmarebooks.com

Space City 6
Copyright © 2014 by Mandy Broughton, Artemis
Greenleaf, Ellen Leventhal, K.C. Maguire, Ellen
Rothberg, Monica Shaughnessy

A Soldier's Gift is a work of historical fiction
based on true events. Names and identifying
details have been changed to protect the privacy
of individuals. Although many events are true,
some are fictitious.

Table of Contents

Fever

Artemis Greenleaf

SEPTEMBER, 1836
Buffalo Bayou, near the burned out ruins of
Harrisburg, Texas

"I don't think this is a good idea, John," Quinn said.

"Of course it is, my good man. Sam Houston is the toast of Texas. A town named after him can't help but succeed. Especially if I can get my fellow representatives in the Congress to make it the capital of the Republic of Texas – indeed, we've already started construction on the capitol building! The Texas government is clamoring for settlers, who will, of course, need a place to live. If we dig out this stagnant old stream, we've got the makings of a grand port," John Allen replied. He gestured to the sluggish bayou in front of them, moving just fast enough to keep the mud churned up in the water and scent the air. A perch glinted silver at the surface as it grabbed a water strider that had ventured too far away from the bank, then disappeared into the murk.

Quinn looked at a pair of yellow eyes floating just above the surface of the opaque water and shrugged. His companion thought it was a basking alligator, a common enough beast in the Gulf Coast swamps, but he knew better.

"Isn't the capital already set up in Galveston? And there's already a major port there, too. Why would any ships come all the way up here?"

"Galveston is the interim capital. We are going to make Houston the permanent one. As for ships coming this far, that's easy. Rail, my good man. This spot is fifty miles closer to existing railways than Galveston. They don't even have a causeway to the island to run a rail line.'

"But there isn't any rail here," Quinn said. The yellow eyes in the murky water at his feet stared balefully up at him.

"Not yet. But it will come. The plans are already in the works." John slapped at a swarm of mosquitoes buzzing around his ears.

"You've taken leave of your senses, John, you and Augustus both."

John laughed loudly, and a snowy egret fled the water for the safety of the trees. "No one thought General Houston could beat Santa Anna, now did they? After the massacres at Goliad and the Alamo, and being outnumbered almost two to one at San Jacinto, only a fool would have bet on Sam Houston. Ha! It's Manifest Destiny, my friend, the will of the Almighty."

Quinn frowned. John Allen squeezed his shoulder. "I've business in Nacogdoches that I must attend to. You won't go wrong buying a parcel of land here, I can assure you. My brother will be most delighted to assist you with the deed while I am away." With that, he mounted his horse and trotted off, crashing noisily through the underbrush.

When the commotion of his passing had quieted, and the twitter of birds and occasional grunting snarls of alligators resumed, the eyes that had been fixed on Quinn rose out of the bayou water. The creature that belonged to the yellow orbs stood upright. Her skin was so dark green as to appear black, unless the sun struck it a certain way, and it was marked by small, vaguely square striations. She was a sobek, and while the ancient Egyptians had painted her kind as alligator-headed people, Quinn knew that modern humans had long ago lost the skill of discernment – they would see nothing but a reptile when they looked at her.

"They must not stay here," she growled, water dripping from her large, re-curved teeth.

"I'm trying to discourage them," Quinn replied.

"Try harder," she answered.

"If you think this is so easy, why don't you have a go?" Quinn snapped.

"Swamp fever has kept humans away for many years with– it was a gift they gave us themselves when they brought others of their kind here in chains to labor in their fields. The fever arrived with them. They come, many die, the survivors leave. So it has been, but I fear that not enough of these invaders will perish if they come in great numbers."

"Perhaps not," Quinn replied.

He was in two minds about humans. His mother had never forgiven them for killing his father, and yet, he'd had a human foundling child named Virginia who was as kind as she was beautiful. He did not know, however, if she was the exception or the norm. His work often brought him into contact with people. Although, they were typically involved with demons, so they were perhaps not the best representatives of their species. Still, he couldn't help but like John Allen.

"It was my understanding that you were here to provide assistance," the sobek woman said.

"I am. I'm just not sure I can accomplish your request."

The alligator fay snarled at him before she slipped back under the murky water of the bayou.

Quinn didn't appreciate being dismissed so harshly, but he didn't fancy going in after her - no telling how many others of her kind were lurking in the muddy water. Besides, the rest of his Mundane Intervention Team - Siobhan, Eoin, Aleksei, and Malik – were waiting for him in Galveston. They had arrived to broker an agreement between the burgeoning human population and the merfolk, who had used the island since it was little more than a sandbar. He shook his head. He hated diplomatic missions, and here he was on not one, but two concurrent ones.

He shifted into the form of a great black horse, and galloped along the waterway. If the bayou was deeper, it would have been faster for him to take his natural kelpie form and swim down to Galveston Bay. Even so, this was not the place to dive in - water fae were notoriously territorial, and the last thing he wanted to do was cause an incident, especially since he was on his own.

Moonlight made the waves shimmer like cut glass, and glinted off the breakers that foamed white before they rolled up onto the beach. The fresh sea breeze was a welcome relief from stifling heat that had oppressed them during the day. Quinn and his team, with the addition of one human in the personage of a Montreal transplant named Michel Branamour Menard, waited at the furthest point on Galveston Island from the busy port, hoping the representative of the West End Sea Tribes Union would arrive soon. She was already late.

Quinn looked at Menard, then at his MIT. Except for Eoin, they could all assume human form, and no one was the wiser. Eoin had his own tricks, however. It would seem that the urisk, who looked human from the waist up, but goatlike from the waist down, would garner a fair amount of attention from panicked humans. But they could stand in front of him and never notice he was there. Unless he desired it. Aleksei, the blue-skinned Lesovik, is what people see when they catch movement out of the corners of their eyes and feel they are being watched in the woods. Unless they look straight at him, in which case he appears to them as a large bush. Even if sighted, recollection of him is slippery, and slides out of the pool of memory like silk over skin. Malik was a djinn, and could take any shape, including none at all, and often did for the sole purpose of amusing himself with pranks against humans. Siobhan could not readily be distinguished by mortal eyes from a comely young lady of the *homo sapiens* species. The tips of her ears were perhaps a little more pointed, and her eyes were slightly larger than the typical human.

On the beach, the tide had risen substantially, and warm water encroached on their gathering.

Quinn looked around and shook his head. "It would seem the merfolk have changed their minds. It is half an hour past the designated time, and their representative has not arrived."

"What does this mean?" snapped Menard.

"It could mean several—" Quinn was cut off by an exquisite and ethereal singing.

Somehow, they had completely missed the approach of the mermaid, because now she sat on the beach not twenty yards away. Her long hair skimmed the sand, and was the same golden brown as the sargassum seaweed that blanketed the beaches in spring. She did not glow, as such, yet even Menard could see her plainly in the dark.

Quinn's team was immune to her song's spell, but they could still appreciate the aching beauty of it while they waited for her to finish. Mr. Menard, on the other hand, was utterly mesmerized.

"Greetings," said Quinn, after the song had stopped.

"Felicitations. Are you the ones that have come to chaffer with me?"

"Indeed," Quinn replied. "And we have brought with us one Michel Menard, who has ambitions of founding a city on your island."

He shook Menard's shoulder, which pulled him out of his trance, then pushed him toward the mermaid. Siobhan rolled her eyes and shook her head.

"*B-b-bon soir, M-M-Madame,*" the man stammered.

"I am called Zara," the mermaid said, casting her silver eyes up and down the quivering human in front of her. "We have no quarrel, in general, with humans. The Karankawa people lived here for many years in peace." When she spoke, her sharp teeth flashed in the moonlight.

"B-b-but there are no Indians here now," Menard said.

"Do you know why that is?" Zara asked.

Menard shook his head. Quinn was unable to determine whether Menard was fearful of Zara, or just dumbfounded by her bare breasts.

"Have you heard tales of the criminal Jean Lafitte?" Zara asked.

Menard nodded.

"Lafitte and his band of miscreants took over the island. They had been here some years when they captured one of our people. She was, of course, reported by the humans to be a Karankawa woman. But when our friends, the tribesmen, tried to free the captive mermaid, they were massacred by the pirates. My people raised the storm that obliterated all of the human habitations and drove them from the island."

Menard took a step back. "*Mon dieu*! You claim to call storms?" His voice had lost its nervous stutter and now contained an edge of skepticism.

"You doubt our abilities? Do not force me to disabuse you of your misapprehensions, sir. As long as your people do not harry or harass my people and do not take more than your fair share of fish, we will not be in conflict. It would be ill-considered for you to do otherwise, Mr. Menard." One of Zara's eyebrows arched as she spoke. "We are fond of this island, and do not wish to damage it, but we will not be mistreated."

"Equinoxes cause the big storms, that is common knowledge – that is why they are called 'equinoctial storms,' after all," Menard said, crossing his arms over his amply-padded chest, as if he had suddenly been injected with a massive dose of courage.

"Is that so, Mr. Menard?"

Suddenly a great howling, as of wind screaming around the corners of a building, rose from the sea and swirled around them. Quinn saw the faces of dozens of merfolk bobbing in the surrounding waters. Aleksei and Eoin chattered nervously together, probably making a contingency plan, given that Aleksei couldn't swim.

Clouds scudded in and smothered the moon. Lightning flashed in the distance. A few fat drops of rain splashed lazily on the group standing on the beach.

"Is it the equinox, Mr. Menard?" Zara asked. Her voice was not loud, but it could clearly be heard over the keening of her people and the howling of the wind.

"*Oui*. Perhaps. The autumnal equinox is in two weeks."

The howling increased. The wind got stronger. Menard's pomaded hair flapped wildly in the squall, and he squinted against the blowing sand. Water ran up the beach and poured over his feet. A clap of thunder boomed above Menard, nearly knocking him to the ground. The force of its rage rippled through the sand. Rain began to torrent down, blown nearly horizontal by the wind.

"*Arrêter!*" Menard shouted. He dropped to his knees and covered his face. "Please stop. I believe you," he whimpered.

The howling ceased and the wind went dead calm. The downpour became a sprinkle, and the lightning stopped flickering across the horizon.

"Do we have an agreement?" Zara asked.

"That my people will leave your people alone, and not overfish? Is that all?"

"That is enough. Break this contract at your peril, Mr. Menard."

With a flick of her tail, Zara pushed herself off of the beach and into the surf.

"That was easy enough," Quinn said. "Now, what are we going to do about the Allen brothers?"

The Mundane Intervention Team had opted to stay in Mrs. Reynaud's boarding house for the few days they'd be in Galveston.

"*Bon matin, mes amis!*" the widow sang at them as they filed into the dining room for breakfast. The smell of fresh-baked bread made

Quinn's stomach protest having to wait another moment for food.

"Good morning," they all responded, but far from in unison.

Mrs. Reynaud disappeared into the kitchen, and moments later, she returned with plates of food. A young lady of African descent helped serve. Quinn could not help but notice that about half of her left ear was missing. When she noticed him looking, she looked away and turned her head. He felt a twinge of guilt for staring at her.

The MIT was famished, the baguettes were hot, and the cheese was delicious. Their hostess even flaunted tradition and provided a jar of fig preserves, probably from the immense fig tree that shaded her front porch, and a large portion of her yard.

A loud banging on the front door interrupted their meal. Mrs. Reynaud's assistant fled, bumping into Siobhan in her haste.

"Open up, Miss Rayno. I believe you got some property of mine," called a loud voice.

"*Monsieur*, I have no property in this house that does not belong to me."

Quinn could see the shadows of three men on the front porch against the lacy curtains.

"Now, Miss Rayno, we don't want to have to break down your door, but we know you got a colored girl in there. She's a runaway slave. Did you not know that, ma'am?"

"I do not know what you are speaking about. Go away. You are disturbing my guests."

Quinn looked around at his team, and his lip twitched into the ghost of a smile. "Invite them in," he said.

"*Je ne comprends pas*. This makes no sense." Mrs. Reynaud replied, shaking her head. Her expression implied that death was both preferable and likely if she complied.

"Your secret is safe with us." Quinn gestured toward the door. "Invite them in."

Cautiously, Mrs. Reynaud opened the door. Three heavily armed men pushed their way inside.

"Jim Bowie, God rest him, always said you were gonna be trouble," the man who had done the shouting at the door said. "Now, if you will kindly turn over our property, we'll be on our way."

"What property is that?" Quinn asked.

One of the men knocked over a porcelain vase filled with flowers. It smashed on the hardwood floor, scattering water, blossoms and fragments of delicate delft blue floral tracery. It was difficult to tell whether the act was deliberate or accidental. He grinned like an oaf either way.

"Colored girl, 'bout so tall..." He raised his hand, palm down, to his chin.

"What color is she?" Siohbhan asked. "Blue? Orange? Green?"

The three men looked at each other, perplexed. "She's the same color as your tea, ma'am," replied the one who had shattered the vase.

"What would you want with her? If such a girl was even here?" Siobhan answered.

The spokesman took a step forward. "Women ought to know their place."

Quinn glanced at Malik. A grin spread over the djinn's face, and his eyes glowed metallic green. A breeze blew across the room, and swirled, faster and faster around the three men. They seemed to be frozen, then disappeared for a few seconds. When they re-appeared, they were not at all themselves.

Instead of three armed white men, there stood three black men, shackled and chained together by iron collars. They started to talk to each other, and discovered, to their obvious horror, that they could only speak Swahili.

Aleksei laughed out loud. "There are three slaves who now look like men that were here, yes?"

Malik nodded.

"I would suggest, Mrs. Reynaud, that you quickly get these three to the auction house. Eoin and Aleksei will help you."

"Non. I would not wish that on even these men. Would you set them free? I'd rather to turn them loose, and let them make their own way."

Malik nodded, and the chains disappeared.

"I hope you know what you're doing," Siobhan said.

Mrs. Reynaud smiled. "*Moi aussi.* Me, too."

The clock struck eight.

"We must be on our way," Quinn said.

Once outside the boarding house, they strolled to the back of the building, away from prying eyes. Six feet pounded by on the sidewalk as the three slavers-cum-slaves fled Mrs. Reynaud's boarding house. Malik waved his hand over the MIT. In an instant, they stood just outside of the building site that was quickly turning into the City of Houston.

"I don't think there's any way to stop the Allen brothers," Quinn said.

"Agreed," replied Eoin.

"You could always eat them," said Malik.

"I'm assuming that was sarcasm," Quinn said. Malik knew full well that, although he was quite capable of dining on humans, they gave Quinn terrible indigestion.

Malik shrugged. "People flow to this place like sand through an hour glass. One grain, more or less makes no difference."

"But what about the sobeks in the bayou?" Siobhan asked.

"Would they consent to being relocated?" Eoin asked.

"Probably not," Quinn replied.

"Yeccchh!"

A man came around the corner, spitting and wiping his mouth on his sleeve. He clutched an empty tin cup in one hand and a roll of papers in his other.

"Are you alright?" Siobhan asked.

"Fine, fine. This milk has gone off. Doesn't last long at all in this heat." He wiped his hand on his pants and extended his hand to Quinn, who was nearest to him. "Gail Borden, surveyor. Pleased to make your acquaintance."

"I believe we've met," Quinn said. "John Allen is an acquaintance of mine, and I call upon him from time to time."

"Ah! So we have. You're that fellow he's been taking around town, aren't you?"

"Yes. These are my associates." He gestured to the rest of his team, but did not go to the trouble of introducing them to Mr. Borden.

Malik pulled a glass bottle from a pocket in his roomy pants and removed the wax seal from the stopper. "Perhaps you should cook it first," he said, taking a drink from the bottle.

"Cook it?...Oh, yes the milk! Grand idea, that. Yes. I shall have to look into it. Now, were you looking for Mr. John Allen?"

"I believe he's gone to Nacogdoches," Quinn replied.

"Augustus is about, somewhere."

"We will locate him, should we require his presence. Thank you."

Borden carried on with his perambulation, and the MIT continued down to the bayou. They had to walk some distance to be out of sight of the construction operations. After calling to the sobeks for nearly an hour and getting no response, Quinn returned his team to the Mundane Activity Monitoring and Intervention Center (MAMIC) in Blackthorne, in the realm of Faery.

MAMIC authorized Quinn to buy a number of plots immediately along Buffalo Bayou to help delay the inevitable conflict between the sobeks and swelling population of the new capital of the Republic of Texas.

August 14, 1838

Quinn found himself back in Houston two years later, at the sweltering apex of summer.

"You know, my good fellow," John Allen said to him, as they walked along the water front. "Those plots you bought are highly coveted. Shall we build on them for you? I'm sure you could put a fine house and a business or two on them. Even with no improvements, they'd still sell for a pretty penny."

"I don't wish to sell them right now," Quinn replied.

"I see." Allen leaned in and lowered his voice. "Confidentially, I've had a change of heart. I have told no one yet. But instead of a port, I believe that the bayou should be filled in."

"Why is that?"

"We had one steamboat come upstream last year. One. And the bayou is so shallow and choked with weeds, that it was a slow and miserable trip. No, I think it will take too much work to make it of any use. Best to fill it in and rid ourselves of these cursed mosquitoes." John slapped one of the offending insects on his arm, and it left a bloody smudge on his arm.

Quinn caught a glimpse of yellow eyes in the murky water, but they were gone so fast he wasn't sure he'd even seen them.

"They seem to be especially bad this summer," John continued.

Quinn noted small red welts, some scratched bloody, on the man's bare forearms. He also noted that John looked thinner and paler than the last time they'd met.

"Well, here we are," John said.

They had arrived at a makeshift tavern, which fit right in with the mostly shanty-town section of city.

"I think it's a terrible idea," Quinn said.

"Having a drink? Surely not."

"No. Filling in the bayou. Are you alright?"

John Allen had crossed his arms over his chest and was rubbing his upper arms as if they were cold.

"I'm, fine," he replied, perhaps with too much emphasis the last word. "Just a little fever. It comes and goes."

As they entered the saloon, John's knees buckled, and Quinn only just caught him before he hit the floor. Quinn laid him out on one of the rickety tables, and the town doctor was called.

His office was only next door, and he arrived within minutes, black bag in hand.

The doctor reeked of cheap whiskey, and Quinn wasn't particularly confident in his abilities. But his diagnosis fit.

"Congestive fever," he said, nodding his head. "This is the third round of it. Every two days he gets a fever, and he's sicker each time."

John Allen, mumbling in his delirium, was carried to his house, but he never woke up.

He died the next day.

Quinn stayed for the funeral. John was only twenty-eight, and had no wife to mourn him. He was laid out in his own parlor, and his mother sat beside the open casket, veiled and dressed in black from head to toe. Quinn shuddered inwardly as he approached to pay his respects – Mrs. Allen wore a large locket with some of John's hair fixed in a basket weave pattern inside. It was a morbidly peculiar habit, these humans had, he thought.

A tall woman, face disguised by a heavy black veil, stood near the back of the room.

"One Allen down, one to go," she said as Quinn got near her. He recognized her as the female sobek from the bayou, although none of the humans seemed to notice her.

"I don't think you'll be able to stop the humans from coming. There are already too many of them, and more arrive every day. For your own safety, I'd like to help relocate your people."

"No."

There was little point in arguing. He sighed softly. "As you wish."

December 22, 1857

"I'm very sorry about your mother," Quinn told the young sobek. He had not yet lost the blotchy cream stripes of a juvenile, and leadership had been thrust upon him by his mother's untimely and fatal interaction with a steamboat.

"Thank you. She never gave up on trying to reclaim our territory from the humans." He looked down and sighed. "Even though many in our tribe had long believed it was a lost cause."

"I understand." Quinn said. Miles of rail lines linking Houston to parts north, west and east were already in operation, and grew longer every day, snuffing out any flicker of hope the sobeks might have had about eradicating the human interlopers from their ancestral home. "A place has been cleared for you, about thirty miles to the southwest of here. There was a human river landing built there, but it has been removed. The Brazos River is slowed by many bends in this area, so it should meet your habitat requirements."

The young sobek nodded slightly and opened the door to what human eyes would perceive as a garden variety stagecoach. It was actually a spatial bubble, which would expand to fit as many as necessary on the inside, but remain the same on the outside.

Quinn held the carriage door open, and the young leader stood opposite him, calling to his people in the croaking, booming language of the sobeks. In small family groups, they rose from the bayou and made their way to the carriage. Heads down, defeated, they walked slowly, and it took longer than Quinn had anticipated to collect them all. When the tear-stained face of the last one disappeared into the inside of the coach, their young leader took one final, sorrowful look around, and climbed in, pulling the door closed behind him.

Quinn climbed into the shotgun seat, and the driver shook the reins and clucked to the horses. Actually, they only looked like horses. In reality, they were a hitch of kelpies – one was even Quinn's cousin – who could do twice the work of a mortal horse in half the time.

It was late afternoon when the coach arrived at its destination, and twilight was already creeping in on this shortest day of the year. The driver pulled up under an immense, Spanish moss-draped live oak tree on the banks of an oxbow lake, formed by a looping bend in the Brazos River. Tall clumps of Texas giant cane shaded the opposite banks and waded partway into the lake. Sabal palms were sprinkled among the oak, hackberry, and pecan trees. A bull alligator, sunning himself just out of the water, looked up cautiously at them.

Quinn opened the stage coach door, and the young leader was the first to emerge.

"It's beautiful!" he exclaimed. "It certainly seems a natural park."

September 8, 1900

"We've got a live one," Quinn said to his team.

They sat around an oaken table in a conference room at the MAMIC headquarters.

"What is it?" Aleksei asked.

"There's a demon, possibly two, who've helped some humans capture a mermaid. We've got to free her, acquire the demons, and neutralize the human witnesses. The method depends on how much they know."

"Where are we off to, then?" Eoin asked.

"Texas. Again," Quinn answered.

"Seems to be a lot going on down there," Siobhan added.

It was still dark when Quinn, Siobhan, Aleksei, Eoin and Malik stepped through the portal onto Galveston Island. Again, they were in the far west section of it.

"It's about time," Zara growled.

"I'm sorry for the delay," Quinn said. "We have been advised that one or more demons is holding one of your tribe captive. Can you apprise us of the situation?"

Anger flashed in Zara's eyes. "Enough talk. You will do something, and do it now, or I will!"

"I understand that you're upset. We will do everything we can to rescue the mermaid. But we've got to contain the demon. Or is it demons? If we don't, this will just recur."

"There are two of them. They've shown some of the humans our abode. But our sister. They've put her on display at the docks."

Quinn and Siobhan exchanged looks. "That complicates things. How many of the towns people have seen her?"

"Most. Perhaps all."

Aleksei swore in Ukranian.

"Do what you will, but know this: a storm has already been called. It is on its way, and is far too big to be stopped," Zara said. "And we would not do so, even if it were possible. These human vermin have been infesting our island for too long. We have been too patient. No more. They have broken the pact, and they will suffer the consequences."

"How long do we have before the storm arrives?" Quinn asked.

"It will arrive this afternoon. The sooner, the better."

"Eoin – I need you to relay this information to Dame Rowan at MAMIC. Aleksei, you're with him. Guard the portal. Go now."

The urisk and the Lesovik headed back to the portal, leaving little goat tracks and odd two-toed footprints in the damp sand.

"Take us to where they are holding your sister," Quinn said to Zara.

The docks heaved with people waiting to pay a nickel each to see the captured mermaid, who was being held in one of the warehouses.

Quinn shook his head. "This makes it much more difficult," he said, surveying the crush of people.

He, Siobhan, and Malik stood at the edge of the crowd. Quinn spotted the first demon right away – it was the one collecting money from the people waiting in line to gawk at the poor captive. Humans, of course, couldn't see that he was a demon – he looked like any other bow-tied salesman to them. But Quinn and company could see its bulging yellow eyes, with their vertical slits, and its grass-colored scales. It hadn't locked onto them yet, but it did pause and wrinkle its nose as if it smelled something offensive.

"Malik, you'll be the hardest for them to detect. Go through the line to check on the mermaid and see if you can find the other demon. If there is an unobtrusive way to free her, do it, but do not call attention to yourself."

Malik nodded.

"And take this trap with you."

Quinn handed over a clear quartz pyramid, the base of which was a little larger than the palm of his hand. Malik tucked it into his voluminous pocket and joined the queue.

"Shall we move to the exit? I think this fellow's a bit suspicious of us," Siobhan said.

They strolled around to the other side of the warehouse to wait for Malik. When he finally emerged, his face was grim.

"She looks very unwell," he said. "Her skin is quite grey, and she is gaunt, as if she has not been eating. I doubt she will survive the night if she's not released."

"What's the layout of the place? How is the mermaid being held?" Quinn asked.

"There is a warehouse with a trap door in the bottom so a barge bearing cargo can pull underneath it and offload the freight directly into storage. The mermaid is secured in a fishing net which dangles through the trap door, half out of the water, so she can be observed. There are other offices and storage areas throughout the building. I tried to slip the rope holding the net and at least lower her into the water, but it is fixed in place with a spell. "

Quinn scowled. "Any sign of the second demon?"

Malik grinned and retrieved the crystal pyramid. A red liquid swirled furiously around inside of it.

"Outstanding," Quinn said. "Take that back to MAMIC for safekeeping, then return here."

Malik left.

Quinn wished the circumstances were different. It was perfect beach weather, warm and sunny. It would have been nice to stroll around with Siobhan and enjoy the day. The breeze had started to pick up, and the water was a little choppy. Although the seagulls were conspicuous by their absence, there was no other hint of what was coming. Something grabbed Quinn's shoulder, hard, and he winced.

Apparently, there was a third demon.

Siobhan pulled a crystal trap out of her handbag, but before she could activate it, the demon whirled around, Quinn still in its deadly grip, and kicked it out of her hand. It landed in the water with a plop and a splash, then sank out of sight.

"Run!" Quinn yelled.

He shifted just enough that his eyes turned black from edge to edge and his teeth went from flat human to sharp kelpie. He spun under the demon's grip and bit down hard on its arm. The beast yowled and let go of Quinn's shoulder. Quinn wiped the demon's black blood off of his face as he fled, following Siobhan.

Demons are not fast runners, and Quinn and Siobhan quickly outpaced it. However, what demons lack in speed, they make up for in stamina. It would hunt relentlessly until it found them.

"Back to the portal. Need reinforcements," Quinn panted as he leaned against the side of a dilapidated wooden house. He brushed against a large rosemary bush, thick trunk gnarled and twisted, and it released its resinous aroma profusely.

"Where is it from here?" Siobhan asked.

"Not sure."

"Hello? Who's there?" called a female voice, cracked with age.

Quinn and Siobhan rounded the corner and discovered an elderly woman with coffee-colored skin and white hair sitting on a porch swing. She wore a pearl earring in her right earlobe, but most of her left ear was missing.

"Sorry ma'am, didn't mean to disturb you," Quinn said. "We'll be on our way now."

"Wait," the woman said. She tilted her head and furrowed her brow. "I know you. It's been a very long time. You look...exactly the same. How can that be?"

"I don't believe we've met," Siobhan answered.

"Yes. We have. I'm sure of it."

"I don't think so," Quinn replied, although there was something vaguely familiar about her. He could hear the slap-slap-slap of the demon's leather boots on the boardwalk, and it would be on them any second now. "We really have to go."

The woman stood up and hobbled the few steps to her front door. "Come inside. Please."

Siobhan nodded to Quinn, and they both ducked into the house. The woman entered behind them and closed the door. She raised her gnarled index finger to her lips, commanding silence. The demon's footsteps were loud now, outside the house. They could hear it snuffling around, trying to catch their scent. Frustrated, it ran on.

"I hate those things," the woman said.

"What things?" Siobhan asked.

"Lizard men. Nasty creatures. That's why I have all the rosemary outside – they hate the smell, and it keeps them away."

Quinn nodded. "Most people can't see them. Odd that you can." Only happens to humans who have been touched by fae. "Thank you for saving us," Quinn said. "But I don't believe I know you." He was only half convinced now that this was true.

"I've waited over sixty years to pay back this debt. I was in Ms. Reynaud's house when the slavers came for me. You stopped them. Both of you."

"You…were the girl?" Siobhan asked.

"Yes. Lucy is my name."

"Lucy, it is so good to meet you again. There isn't much time. You have to gather any friends and family that you care about, and get off the island. Today. Now. There's a storm coming, and it's going to be a bad one. We have to go. So do you," Quinn said.

Lucy nodded. "I guess Dr. Cline was right about his hurricane warning, then."

By the time that Quinn and Siobhan made their way to the portal and rendezvoused with Eoin, Aleksei and Malik, the afternoon shadows were just beginning to lengthen. The wind had kicked up and the tide was high, higher than normal. To the east and south, the sky was black with rain. Away from the town, they could hear the wrothful howling of the merfolk, calling the storm, making it stronger, pouring their rage into it. They were almost out of time to capture the remaining two demons.

With a blink of his eye, Malik took them back to the docks. The earlier crowds had dispersed, no doubt battening down their hatches, for all the good it would do them, against the approaching storm. Cautiously, expecting a trap, they neared the warehouse. What they heard was someone crying, wailing in grief. Inside the warehouse, they found Zara underneath the dock, clinging to the netting that held the captured mermaid. The captive lay limply on the bottom of the net, arms and hair drifting in the current. The rising water had floated the corpse nearly up into the trap door, and the high swells occasionally pushed her partially through it.

Zara's head jerked up as they entered. "They have killed her! They will pay for this. They. Will. Pay." She turned and dove into the water, splashing them with a contemptuous flick of her tail.

A door slammed behind them, in the depths of the warehouse. They all ducked behind wooden crates or bales of cotton, whichever was closest to each.

"Talco?" a demon's gravelly voice called.

Malik eased a quartz demon trap out of his pocket and handed it to Eoin, who silently twisted the top half of it open.

The demon never knew what hit him as he came through the door. By the time he realized he'd been ambushed, it was too late, and he was locked inside the crystal. Malik tucked the pyramid away.

"Nooo!" screeched a deep, raspy voice.

The demon that had been collecting money to see the mermaid came roaring up at them.

Malik tried stunning it with a spell, but the demon swiped his magic to the side. Aleksei put his head down and drove his shoulder into the demon's midsection with enough force to knock the wind out of him. As he staggered back, Eoin grabbed one of his arms, while Aleksei wrapped his own arms around the demon's opposite leg. Demon claws raked Aleksei's back and head, and deep blue blood oozed from the scratches. Malik grabbed at the flailing claws as the demon lifted Eoin off his feet with the arm that the urisk was attempting to control. The demon would not be laid down on the floor, so Quinn grabbed his foot. He was rewarded with a kick in the face hard enough to bloody his lip, but he and Aleksei were able to yank its feet out from under it. Taking Eoin and Malik with him, the demon thudded to the floor with a loud "Ooof!" Finally, they pinned him to the floor, barely.

Rain pounded the windows, increasing in fury. Wind moaned across the roof, pelting the building with small, forsaken items. Surging water splashed through the open trap door, pushing the cargo net with the dead mermaid onto the warehouse floor.

"We've got to get out of here. Who has a trap?" Quinn asked, wiping blood from his mouth.

No one, it turned out.

"I really hate doing this," Siobhan said, She pulled a golden dagger from her belt. The demon fought – it knew what was coming. "I'm so sorry. If there was any other way..." she said. Then she raised her hand and drove the dagger deep into its heart. The demon bellowed, then exploded in a cloud of noisome ash.

"Go, go, go! We have to get to the portal, now," Quinn called.

The five fae raced out of the warehouse. The furious wind ripped shingles from the roof, and planks from the walls, and hurled them after the MIT with a vengeance.

Behind them, in the collapsing warehouse, a boy began to wail for the father whose slaughter he had just witnessed through a crack in cargo area door.

"Shhh, Balcones. If you want to live long enough for revenge, we have to go," his scaly mother called to him.

The seeds of vengeance took root then, in what passes for a demon's heart, and demanded to be watered with the blood of his enemies. Pain and anger fused into incandescent rage, burning him from the inside out, just like malaria that had consumed John Allen.

"Yes, Mother," he answered, his yellow eyes fever-bright.

A Soldier's Gift

Ellen Leventhal

THERE WEREN'T A LOT of ham sandwiches and tuna casseroles in Washington Terrace. But what it lacked in white bread and baked cheese casseroles, it made up for in brisket, matzah ball soup, and poppy seed rolls. Washington Terrace was a neighborhood of immigrants.

New York had enough poor refugees of their own, so between 1907 and 1914, a few thousand of the huddled masses got shipped to Galveston, Texas. Elias Waring and Carrie Bloom's parents were among the several thousand refugees who, instead of seeing Lady

Liberty's torch upon arrival, landed on the small barrier island off the Texas coast. Although many of the newly arrived Jewish families found themselves selling bananas and tin pots from pushcarts in places like Waco and Tyler, Elias and Carrie's parents wanted more. They were among those who made their way across the bay to Houston where they hoped to find greater opportunity and a decent place to raise their children. And it was there that Elias and Carrie began their story.

September 25, 1941
Houston, TX

Elias walked the familiar streets to Carrie's house. He wasn't sure if it was the oppressive heat, the darkness, or the snippet of grim news coming out of Europe that tore at him the most. The sounds of rebuilding...hammering, sawing, and a bit of swearing... drifted through the air. Houston was cleaning up after another hurricane, but Elias Waring's thoughts were on a different type of storm.

Jumping over puddles of stagnant water, he ran the last few feet to Carrie's house. The humidity was stifling and mosquitos dive bombed him with each step. He was used to it, though. Having grown up in a city built on bayous and swamps, this was just a part of life.

Carrie burst out the door before Elias could climb the four broken concrete steps to her house. "Let's get out of here," she said.

"You really want to walk outside in this mess?" Elias asked.

"You know me," Carrie said. "I love a challenge!"

"I guess you do. I remember when you insisted that you could run faster than any boy on the street. And you were right," Elias said.

"And I didn't care one bit that Ralphy Gold cried about it," she said. They took hands and smiled. "I'm glad we're such good friends, Elias."

"And I'm glad you finally agreed to be *more* than friends after years of chasing you!" he said. They both laughed.

"It's good to see you laugh, Elias. It's been a while," Carrie said.

"Tell me the real reason you wanted to leave the house. I know it wasn't just to trudge around in mud," said Elias.

"Privacy, I guess," she answered. "And I need to get away from what's going on inside. Mrs. Boden is in there, and she's crying again. Mother is trying to calm her, but it doesn't seem to be working. How could it? Mother doesn't really know what to say."

"It's scary, Car. You know that a lot of the Boden family is still over there,"

"Do you think it's as bad as they say?"

"It's been two years since Hitler invaded Poland, and now he's trying for all of Europe. Maybe even the world. And Roosevelt is turning a deaf ear," Elias said.

"That's not completely true. We send arms to the Allies. It's just that nobody here wants to go to war," Carrie said.

"Sure, after all, we just finished 'The War to End All Wars'," Elias added, rolling his eyes.

Stepping over lumber, they walked in silence for a bit. The moon peeked out from behind a cloud, but didn't lend much light. Elias aimed his flashlight in front of them, and smalls shards of broken glass glistened as if leading the way.

Carrie broke the silence. "Our own relatives were lucky enough to get out of Europe while the getting was good."

"Not all," Elias whispered.

Carrie's stomach lurched. How could she be so insensitive? "I'm sorry, Elias. I sometimes forget that you still have family there," she said.

"My mother used to get letters from her cousins, but they've completely stopped. We haven't heard from them in a long time. Maybe they're ok. I don't know. And it….." Elias stopped mid-sentence, not knowing how to continue.

As they walked past open windows, the pair could hear snippets of conversation. Some of it was in Yiddish, and although they didn't understand a lot, they knew enough.

"It's like before. In the Old Country."

"Only this time it's worse, if that's possible!"

"How much worse can it be? The pogroms….there can be nothing worse!"

"And for the ones not being rounded up yet, try to get a visa to come here! They won't let you! Lady Liberty just sits in the water laughing!"

"Give us your tired, your poor, but not your persecuted Jews!"

"Emma Lazarus wrote that poem. Emma Lazarus, a Jew herself!"

"Lord! It sounds like we're living in a *shtetl* here!" said Elias. "Our own little Texas ghetto."

Slogging through muddy streets, the couple made their way to a park where they found a semi-dry bench. "Do you think that Roosevelt will change his mind? Do you think the US will enter the war?" asked Carrie settling herself on the seat.

"I don't know, but if he does, I'll be the first one to enlist," answered Elias.

"But you want to be a lawyer. The war will change that."

"How?" he asked. He kicked a fallen branch. "We're not in the war now, and I'm just a tailor's son working in a tailor's shop!"

Always feisty, Elias had become quick tempered over the last few months. It was as if his own personal storm was brewing just below the surface.

The news coming out of Europe disturbed everyone. Talk of the war and the possibility of U.S involvement took over evening conversation everywhere from River Oaks to Freedman's Town. But for the residents of Washington Terrace, it was personal. Hitler was building more gas chambers and crematoriums, and more families like the Warings waited for news that never came.

"The world is a mess," Elias complained. "Europe and Asia are falling apart, people are getting murdered for no reason, and I'm here ironing rich people's clothes. Something's not right."

"I know. I know. Things will change. I feel it," answered Carrie.

December 8, 1941
Houston, Texas

Boys barely old enough to shave circled Army Enlistment Centers throughout the country. Among the boys chomping at the bit to get into a center in Houston, was a dark eyed, intense, tailor's son.

Once inside the Enlistment Station, Elias heard someone call his name. "Hey, Elias! I guess you're not going to be that lawyer now!" He looked across the room to see the lanky figure of Izzy Green, the forward on his YMHA basketball team.

"I guess not, but maybe I can save the world instead," he answered with a nervous laugh.

Elias knew his dreams would be on hold or totally destroyed. But becoming a lawyer was less important to him now. He thought about Carrie, and he knew she would understand. His Carrie with the trusting eyes. She would be proud of him. Five minutes before closing time, Elias Waring scribbled his name on the forms, slammed down his pen, and saluted. He couldn't wait to take the Oath of Enlistment.

August, 1942
Camp Polk, Louisiana

"Hey Jew Boy! You up for this? I wouldn't want you to break your glasses or anything." Elias looked up from his bunk and put the letter from Carrie down. A boy-stocky build, round face, and smelling vaguely of tobacco. "Hey Jew boy! I'm talking to you!"

Elias knew his kind; this was nothing new. He got up from his bunk and walked away. "Talk to Roosevelt then, if you don't want to go. No skin off my back," he called over his shoulder.

"We're going over there to save the asses of your relatives, and you're just turning away? Maybe Hitler does need to clean up a little!"

Elias was not religious, and in the past, being Jewish meant nothing to him. He could be Buddhist for all he cared. But now it mattered. He pivoted, stepped towards the laughing bully, and slugged him soundly in the face. That was the first of many army scuffles.

March 30, 1943
Houston, TX
"*Mazel Tov!*"

Elias stomped on the glass signifying the end of the marriage ceremony. The room erupted in cheers. Elias took Carrie's hand.

"I can't believe we finally did it," Carrie whispered to Elias.

"I can't believe we waited so long," he answered.

"Our lives are like this glass," Carrie said. "Fragile."

"I know," he answered. "I'll be getting my orders to ship out overseas soon. But let's be happy now."

Elias would have been happy taking his bride to City Hall, getting married, and then hopping in the car to take a little honeymoon. There wasn't time or money for much, but a buddy in Dallas set them up in a nice hotel and got them dinner reservations at a fancy restaurant. After that, they'd take a train to California, where Elias was stationed.

But at the Blooms' insistence, the couple found themselves exchanging vows in Carrie's aunt's cramped living room. The wedding canopy, made from her grandfather's *tallis*, filled most of the space at the front. Carrie reached up to touch the silky texture and twirl the fringes. She never knew her grandfather, but she could feel his presence.

Elias had never worn a prayer shawl and felt uncomfortable standing under one. The rabbi conducted most of the ceremony in Hebrew which Elias didn't understand, but when Carrie's cousin sang, *Ani le, le dodi le* he understood all he needed to. *I am my beloved's and my beloved is mine.*

As the room echoed with *Mazel Tovs* and *L'Chiams, a* sudden clap of thunder shook the China, and the room went dark. Rain pounded the roof with an intensity that made children cling to their mothers' skirts. Ethel Waring wrung her hands. Carrie looked toward her new mother-in-law and understood. She hoped that the weather wasn't a portent of things to come.

December 10, 1944
France

"Well, Merry Christmas, Tex," sang gunner, Jose Martinez. "I know it's not really Christmas yet, and you probably don't even care, but what the hell?

"Yeah, that's swell. Let's have an early Christmas this year." Elias said. "We don't know if we'll be alive for the real one so, yeah, let's celebrate."

"All I could find was this tea that our French friends left us," drawled tank driver, Bobby Johnson. "And some stale biscuits."

"That's ok, Bobby," said Martinez. "We'll pretend its whisky and caviar." A fresh faced southern boy, Bobby was the baby of the group. He had his first taste of whisky with his army buddies.

The group holed up in an old farm house and waited for orders. There was no heat, so they made due with blankets they found in a closet. Bow gunner, Billy O'Brian, waved his fingers. "You think if my fingers come off from the cold, they'll send me home?"

"You wish," said Martinez. "They'll find someone else's fingers, sew them on you, and then send you back into combat. That's the American way, right, Lieutenant?"

Elias, commander of the platoon, laughed. "Maybe, Martinez. Maybe. It's a lot different here than at Camp Cooke, huh? Now that was a nice gig."

"Yeah, the nice weather and some movie stars," Martinez added.

"And the women....oh boy, there were some good looking women out there," said O'Brian.

"We're in France, now. You know what they say about French women. Maybe we'll get lucky, Billy Boy," said Martinez. "Those other guys can sigh over pictures of their stateside sweeties, but we are footloose and fancy free!"

Laughing at the absurdity of that statement, they filled their tin cups. They were here to work, not play, and they knew it. The 42nd Tank Battalion, Company D would finish this war and assure an Allied victory.

"Merry Christmas!" they said in unison.

December 31, 1944
Rechival, Belgium

Elias Waring's tank battalion crossed into Belgium and was on alert. The *Battle of the Bulge* was in full swing, and they were about to enter the fray. Sharing cramped quarters in a rundown barn in Rechival, didn't help their already tense mood. The snow was heavy and falling sideways, the temperature was below zero, and the only thing the men knew for sure was that death was knocking at the door.

"Man, I remember some great New Year's Eve parties at home," sighed Martinez.

"And here I am, sharing my evening with you slobs. I could be with my honey doing what honeys do," said Johnson.

"And, you, Jew Boy Tex, always mooning over that picture," added O'Brian.

"That's *Lieutenant* Jew Boy Tex to you," Elias laughed and put Carrie's picture down. He had looked at it so many times that his fingerprints were now part of the background.

"You act like it's the God damned Holy Grail," said O' Brian.

"You bet I do!" said Elias. "It's better than the Holy Grail to me. It's what's getting me out of here alive.

Martinez found an old bottle of Scotch that someone had left in the barn. He filled his friends' cups and raised his. "To us!" he shouted as he downed a shot from a dirty tin cup.

"To us," the others murmured.

"L'Chiam!" added Elias. It was one of the few times that Elias drew attention to his Jewish heritage. "It means 'to life'."

December 31, 1944
Houston, TX

Christmas vacation was almost over for Carrie who found a job teaching at her old school. Elias had been overseas for a few months now, and Carrie decided it made sense for her to move back home for a while.

"So do you like being home?" Carrie's friend, Dotty, asked. They were walking home from helping at the Red Cross.

"It makes sense, I guess. Although nothing these days really makes sense," she answered. "I wish I could do more. Elias is over there, and I'm here doing nothing! Staying in Houston rolling bandages is not my idea of helping the war effort."

"I bet this is the last New Year's Eve that we'll be at war!" Dotty flashed a smile. Carrie resented Dotty's cheerfulness.

"I hope so," Carrie muttered.

The friends parted at Almeda St. "Happy New Year, Car," Dotty said. "It will be a good year, I know it."

"Happy New Year to you too. I hope you're right."

When Carrie got home, she picked up Elias's latest letter. She had read it before, but even though the words did not bring her comfort, holding it felt right.

My Dearest Carrie,

I cannot tell you a lot, but I will tell you that things are heating up here. Don't worry, I'll be home, but I don't know when. We are in Belgium now, and if you listen to the news, you know we will be in heavy battle. Our orders have come. We're going in soon, and once we do, I don't know how much I will be able to write.

Thank Mom for the blanket. It came in handy. And please take care of her for me, ok? She's not as strong as you. I will see you again. I love you.

Forever,

E

The family spent a quiet New Year's Eve together. Carrie put some music on hoping to keep her mind occupied. She took a sip of the overly sweet wine they shared. Wrinkling her nose, she walked outside to get some fresh air. Looking up and down the street, Carrie counted the Gold Stars hanging in her neighbors' windows. Every day another family heard "the worst." The knot in her stomach tightened, and she went back inside.

"L'Chaim! This is the year we'll get our boy home!" said Elias's father, David. He lifted his glass.

Carrie's father, Sam, chimed in. "I'll drink to that!"

Carrie slept fitfully that night. Turning over, she caught a glimpse of the clock on her night stand. Squinting to adjust to the dark, she saw that it was 3:00 A.M.... January 1, ten o'clock in the morning in Belgium. Elias would be in battle now. Despite the warm quilts, she shivered. Breaking down into deep sobs, she reached for the sedative the doctor prescribed, but could barely lift it to her mouth.

January 1, 1945
Rechival, Belgium

As his tank lumbered through rough terrain, Elias glanced at Carrie's picture. The crew could hear the captain telling them to move on. Everything was clear. No problem. "Cap says to keep moving," said Elias, "so let's go."

"Is he crazy? They're all around us!" shouted O' Brian.

"Keep going!" ordered Elias.

"There's no way! The Krauts are surrounding us." Martinez yelled. The snow obscured their vision, but their other senses were strong. German tanks were to the right, left, and behind them.

"Do your job, soldier!" ordered Elias. "We're clearing the road to Bastogne so our guys can end this damn war!"

Screams in both English and German mingled with the howling wind and the non-stop tank fire. The snow, once pristinely white was now red. Bodies dotted the landscape, but there was no time to mourn.

Elias turned to deliver an order, but before he could get the words out, a figure in the distance caught his eye. "Stop! He's an American. We need to get him!"

O'Brian answered. "It's too late for him, Lieutenant; we need to get out of here."

"He's moving. He's still alive! I'll get him!" Elias ordered Johnson to stop the tank, and amid German fire, he jumped off and ran towards the wounded man. With the driving snow and wind, Elias had a hard time seeing, but the bone sticking out of the soldier's leg couldn't be missed. The sound of tank fire was deafening, but Elias called to the man.

"I got you, soldier, I got you!" he shouted. Falling into the snow, Elias doubled over. He was hit. He slowed down, but fought the stabbing pain in his left arm. Wincing he scooped up the soldier with his good arm and dragged him through bloody snow towards his tank.

Fighting the driving snow, enemy tanks, and pain, Elias reached the tank with the wounded stranger. Letting out a scream, he hoisted the man onto the tank.

"He won't survive," said Martinez as they wrapped his wound. "The leg is torn to bits. I've never seen anything like this. His breathing is shallow."

"You're probably right," answered Elias. "But at least he'll die warm. We can't leave him to freeze to death out here."

"You're crazy, but I guess some would call you a hero after this," said Martinez.

"I could have been faster," Elias muttered. "You're no hero when the man dies."

As they rolled into the aid station, medics ran out to meet the tank. Looking at the wounded soldier, they shook their head and gathered him up.

"What about the lieutenant?" Martinez asked.

"I'm fine," said Elias. "Let's go."

"You *will* be fine, in a minute," a medic answered as he dug shrapnel out of Elias's arm.

"Let's go!" Elias said after he was cleaned and wrapped up.

"Back out there? Are you crazy? Sir?" asked Martinez. "We're moving right into the lion's den."

"We're gonna die anyway," said O' Brian. "But we can take as many Krauts with us as we can."

Elias had never believed in God, but he found himself praying that there was one. With a leap of faith, he ordered the tank to move forward.

"We can't get through here," Johnson reported. "We can't see past this hedgerow. These things have eaten tanks before."

"You can bet the enemy will be behind them," added Martinez.

"Push through!" ordered Elias.

"Yes sir," answered Johnson. "Nothing matters now anyway."

They pushed through the hedgerow only to findthemselves at the bottom of a deep tank trap. Johnson maneuvered the tank, pushing back and forth, breaking up ground, until he was finally able to drive forward out of the trap.

But it wasn't over. "Look out!" called O'Brien. As they made their way out of the trap, a German Self Propelled anti-tank gun rumbled towards them.

"Hard left!" Elias commanded. "Now hard right!" Their small tank was shaking, but with Elias's leadership, they wended their away from the gun's muzzle.

"Whee hoo, Tex! We did it!" called Johnson. "We're alive!

"It's not over yet," said Elias. "We're still surrounded." Light to begin with, the tank was in bad shape. With its wobbly track and broken turret, it would be like a toy car to the Germans. Slipping and sliding on the ice, Johnson turned in circles, trying to find a spot to get off a shot. With a German tank in sight, Martinez aimed and fired six or seven times.

"My shots bounce right off," Martinez told the others.

"They're armor piercing missles, it's got to work!" O'Brian yelled from the back of the tank.

Projectiles flew back and forth. It was now a game of who could maneuver their tanks the best. With a sharp turn of the tank, Martinez was able to get off the perfect shot. The American's 37 mm projectiles hit the German tank's engine compartment bringing the enemy tank to a halt. Black smoke surrounded it. It wasn't going anywhere.

The group whooped like school boys. And then their luck ran out. Flames shot up from the back of their tank.

"We've been hit! Get out!" ordered Elias. "Dive!" he yelled. Deep in the snow, he watched as his his tank became engulfed in flames. Elias thought he saw something or someone running back towards the burning tank. And then it all went dark.

January 1, 1945
Houston, Texas

It had been a tradition in the past, and Ethel Waring decided war or no war, she would have friends and family in to celebrate the New Year. It might keep her mind off her son.

Carrie and her parents were the first ones to arrive. "You're pale, sweetheart," Sam said to his daughter as they walked into the house. "Are you ok?"

"I'm fine," she answered. Once she sat down, she kept her hands busy knitting, hoping nobody would notice them shaking. No sense worrying anyone else.

Ethel baked cookies and passed them around. "I'm sorry these cookies don't taste like they should," she said. "With sugar rationing, well, you know. I tried my best."

"Have you heard from your boy lately?" Mrs. Albert asked.

"He's fighting in the Battle of the Bulge," answered Dotty. "He can't write every day." Dotty held her friend's hand and squeezed it. Dotty had become a part of the family, and Carrie was grateful for her friendship.

"And Ethel, what about your family in Poland?" Have you heard from them?" Mrs. Albert continued. Ethel Waring looked down at her dress and shrugged her tired shoulders.

Still passing cookies around, she said, "Sorry I couldn't make my babka," Rationing, you know."

January 3, 1945
Houston, TX

Carrie was not sleeping or eating. Her clothes hung on her, and the dark circles under her eyes aged her.

Helping her mother clean up from dinner, she could barely stand. "I know something terrible happened," she said under her breath. Despite the unusually cool winter, beads of sweat dotted her face.

"We haven't heard anything, darling. Why are you so worried?" asked Helen.

"I just know," Carrie said.

They were in the kitchen when they heard the three chimes of the doorbell above the din of clanging dishes. Carrie held her breath.

Holding her daughter close, Helen said, "You don't know."

"I do," answered Carrie. "I do."

Gathering her courage, Carrie went to the door. "Who is it?" she asked, even though she knew.

"Department of the Army, M'am. Are you Mrs. Waring?"

Carrie's hands shook, but somehow she was able to sign for the letter. She stumbled back to the living room. Opening it slowly, her chest heaved and her sobbing got louder.

"Oh God!" she cried. "He's alive. He's hurt bad, but he's alive."

January, 15 1945
Austria

Elias blinked and flexed his swollen feet. Groaning, he managed to push his legs over the bed. The bandages around his abdomen were tight, and the slightly metallic smell of blood and burnt tissue made his stomach roil. He was hurt, but somehow he had survived. "I saw the tank explode. And then the Germans, and Jesus, how am I alive? Where am I?"

"An aid station. You'll be ok," answered a medic. "You've been here a while."

"Someone was running back towards the tank. My men, are they gone?" asked Elias.

"Your men made it," the medic said. "In fact, they say you saved their lives with your quick thinking."

"I don't remember much…except that guy we brought in. The one with the bone sticking out of his leg. I couldn't help him. I tried, but I couldn't help him," Elias mumbled. "He's dead. I wasn't fast enough. And then the explosion. So many bodies. We should all be dead."

"But you're not. You'll be ok now, soldier," the medic assured him.

"New Year's Day. What happened?" asked Elias.

The medic looked down at the floor. "It was bad," he said.

"Tell me," Elias continued.

The medic told Elias the grim statistics. "Company D, 42nd tank battalion lost twelve of fifteen tanks. And the men in them."

Elias put his head in his hands.

"Hey! Lieutenant! You're back in the land of the living." Elias looked toward the voice. Standing in the doorway was a pale, bandaged Billy O'Brian.

"Wait! It was you! You went back and…..what's going on here?" asked Elias.

O'Brian held something in his hand. "It's a little burnt around the edges, but I think you'll want this. Amid the ashes in that tank, the only thing that survived was the dog-eared picture of Carrie."

And then Elias wept.

February 6, 1945
Houston, TX

Settling into a window seat in her bedroom, Carrie took out the letter. She read it aloud to Dotty.

My Dearest,

I hate being in this bed. It's been over a month, and they tell me that I was unconscious most of the time. Although I felt some pain, it was bearable, and as the docs say, I floated in and out.

I can handle the physical pain, and I am slowly regaining my strength. But there is so much sadness here. First and foremost, there is the pain of not seeing you. But my darling, I know we will see each other again. And the pain of knowing I could have done more to help my fellow soldiers. I will live

*with that forever. On a brighter side, they're telling
me that the Allies put a nail in Hitler's coffin. I
should be home with you again soon.*

All my love,

E

"You should be so proud of Elias," said
Dotty.

"I am, but this thing isn't over. And my
mother-in-law cries all day. Not just for Elias,
but for all the GIs. And for her cousins.
Probably all murdered in the camps. I don't
know if it will ever be over," said Carrie.

"All we can do is hope," replied her
friend.

February 7, 1945
Austria

Elias bolted up in his bed and began
barking out orders.

"*I got you, soldier! I got you!*"

"You're having that dream again,
Lieutenant." A nurse was there when he opened
his eyes. "Do you want to talk about it?"

"The man comes back. His bones are protruding, and he's telling me I could have saved him, but I wasn't fast enough."

"You did your best," the nurse whispered.

Elias fell back into a troubled sleep, but an unfamiliar booming voice awoke him at dawn.

"That son of a bitch is almost done, and we have a chance to save some of those poor wretches in the camps!" An imposing figure walked into the aid station. Elias recognized him as one of General Patton's closest aids.

Elias pushed himself up, rocked a bit, and finally stood up holding on to a rickety IV pole. "Count me in. I have to go!" he shouted.

"You can barely move," said the man and marched away just as suddenly as he came in. With a parting glace at Elias, he said, "Waring, you gotta walk before you can help anyone else. And maybe you need to see the shrink. I hear you're waking everyone up at night."

With the pain still searing though his body, Elias pushed himself every day. The muscles in his arms rippled as he did pull ups, and his legs shook with each shaky step. But every day he worked out, took his meds, and of course, wrote to Carrie.

May 1, 1945
Linz, Austria

Elias and his crew were at a rest stop at the top of a hill waiting for orders. He had been back in action for a while now and felt ready for what would come next. "Hand me a smoke, would you?"

Bobby Johnson took a cigarette out of his pocket.

"Look at this," Johnson said scanning the view. "Neat little houses, a flowing river, and murderous Nazis inside playing cards."

Taking a drag of the cigarette, Elias said, "While we sit up here, they're murdering people in ovens someone over those next few hills. Can't be more than ten miles away. Something's got to happen."

"And you, Mr. Big Shot, will get to lead a task force and do something about it," O'Brian said, slapping Elias on the back.

"But when? What's taking them so long to give us our orders?" he asked.

The sun set, and the group settled in to get some rest. Elias was reading *Stars and Stripes* when he heard that booming voice again. "Hey Waring! It's time. If you want to take one of those task forces into the camps, get your unit together and get your asses moving. We're about ready to roll out. And that's from Patton himself!"

May 5, 1945
Mauthausen, Austria

A tailor's son from Houston, Texas commanded the lead tank. Entering the town of Mauthausen, the odor of rotting flesh was overwhelming. His tank approached the top of a hill when an old man stepped out from behind the trees. He held up his hand, bringing the entire column to a standstill. Looking straight through Elias with piercing blue eyes, he spoke in Yiddish. Elias knew just enough of the language to understand what he said. "You're too late. They are all burned."

Nonetheless, tanks continued up the last hill and stopped at the top. "It looks like something out of a movie," said Martinez with a catch in his voice. In front of them, was the proof. The proof that people were being systematically murdered. On command, the tanks pushed through the entrance of the stone fortress. There were clothes and pieces of human tissue still stuck to the electric fence around the perimeter. Were they too late? Hundreds of bodies were stacked up like cordwood. Full grown men weighing 50, 60, or 70 pounds was the rule, not the exception. Prisoners, most unable to stand on their own, clawed their way into the American tanks shrieking and wailing.

A walking skeleton called to Elias with his hand outstretched. Wiping his eyes, Elias gave the prisoner a candy bar. Following Elias's lead, soldiers from different platoons gave out chocolate and other food hoping that it would give the prisoners some strength. But to their horror, this made things even worse. Bobby Johnson was the first to notice it. "We're killing them!" he hollered. "Oh my God, we're killing them. They can't stop vomiting!"

The stench of death was overwhelming. Smoke from the crematorium still formed a terrible mist in the air. Forcing themselves to move further into the interior, the men looked down into the quarry and saw the bodies that didn't make it to the crematorium. Hardened soldiers who thought they had seen it all retched and wept.

Nothing made sense. Standing inside the fortress at the top of that hill, Elias looked over the stone walls down at the town. He saw houses and gardens and children playing. The children reminded him of Carrie's students. And of Carrie.   But inside this hilltop torture chamber, just a mile away from the playing children, there were children too. Only they were not playing. Those who were not dead, were close to it. They never got a chance to be children.

Elias and his men lifted prisoner upon prisoner onto the tank. As he carried one woman, she screamed out her last breath pointing to something. Elias looked as he lay the now dead woman on the ground. A German guard cowering in a corner.

The forearm of Elias's rifle against his head, the guard pleaded. "I was just following orders! Doing my job!

Elias took his Star of David out of his shirt, waved it in the guard's face, and said, "And now I'm about to do my job!"

Jan 1, 1985
Houston, TX

"Have you spoken to the guys yet today?" Carrie asked.

"Just O'Brian so far," answered Elias. With the details of January 1, 1945 etched in their collective memories, the tank crew spoke every New Year's Day. Elias's shoulders slumped, and he retreated to the den. Carrie didn't begrudge her husband his New Year's phone reunions. She was glad they were all in touch, but she wished this day wasn't so hard on him.

"The kids are coming over soon, and we need you here with us, not in Belgium," Carrie said. And then taking his hand, she quietly added, "Or even Austria. Just here in Texas. At home with us."

"You weren't there, and you'll never understand," said Elias brusquely.

"That's true, I won't. But look at all the good work you do now! You speak about the horrors of the Holocaust, and you help teach its lessons." Carrie's voice was pleading. "I understand you have terrible memories. I'm the one who is here when after forty years you still wake up screaming. It's over. The ones who died, the camps. It's all over. Let it go."

Elias softened and took her other hand. He couldn't help thinking about all those who didn't make it. Especially those in the camps, the hundreds who died in in the snow in Belgium, and the man who he could have saved. If only he was faster.

January 12, 1985
Houston, TX

The Law Office of Elias Waring, Esq. was unusually quiet. Elias finished the last brief of the day, and began to gather his things. Looking forward to seeing the grandkids at their weekly family dinner at Ninfas, Elias had one foot out the door when the phone rang. Remembering his secretary had left, he answered the phone.

"Elias Waring."

"Is this Elias Waring?"

"Yeah, buddy, I said that's who I am. Who is this?" Elias was agitated. Who was this joker keeping him here?

"I saw your name in the paper and tracked you down," answered the voice on the other end.

"Who *are* you?" Elias asked.

"Do you remember Jan.1, 1945?"

Elias paled and asked, "Is this a joke? If it is, it's sick."

"Do you remember carrying a guy to safety?"

Elias grabbed his chair and sank down into it. "Pretty sure that poor guy died before anyone could even get to him. So no, I didn't carry anyone to safety. Who *are* you?"

"My name is Jake Brown. Thanks, Lieutenant. I made it. I survived."

January 20, 1985
Houston, TX

"I'll have a chicken salad on pumpernickel, please," Elias said to the waitress.

"Your usual, huh?" asked the waitress with a smile.

"Today is anything but usual," he answered.

Stirring his coffee with jittery hands, Elias glanced around the crowded bagel shop. How would he know Jake?

And then he heard it. "I'd know you anywhere, Lieutenant," called an unfamiliar voice.

Elias looked up to see a man limping towards him with arms wide open.

"I saw your picture in the paper," said Jake.

The two soldiers hugged.

"How is this possible? How did you survive?" asked Elias.

"You saved me, you know that."

Feb. 14, 1985
Houston, TX
You are my sunshine, my only sunshine........

Carrie and Elias squeezed into chairs made for much smaller rumps, but beamed as their grandson sang with his class. Jake and his wife were next to them.

In a another twist of fate, Elias and Jake lived only five minutes apart; one in Maplewood and one in Meyerland. Their grandchildren were in the same pre-school class.

"Can you believe this?" Jake's wife softly asked as the children sang. "Elias, if it wasn't for you, none of this would be possible. Jake would not have survived and……." Her voice cracked. She couldn't go on.

After all the cupcakes had been eaten, the teacher began to talk to the grandparents. Elias wasn't listening to what she said, but her accent brought unwanted memories to the surface

"She's a Holocaust survivor," whispered one of the other grandparents. Carrie looked at Elias.

As everyone was gathering up their children to leave, Elias spoke to the teacher. "I hope I'm not being too personal, but I heard you were a Survivor. May I ask what camp?"

Before she could answer, his grandson ran into his teacher's arms. "I love you, Mrs. Burger!"

She hugged him and said, "I love you too, Daniel." Then she looked at Elias and answered his question. "Mauthausen," she said. "Why do you ask?"

Killer Jack

Monica Shaughnessy

HARDY THIBAULT ALWAYS DID as he was told, and his wife, Vera, did most of the telling. When she instructed him to climb on the roof and trim their live oaks during last Monday's lightning storm, he climbed. When she ordered him to swim in the swirling, debris-choked waters of Brays Bayou to retrieve her flip-flop the next morning, he swam. When she demanded he park on the narrow shoulder of I-10 a few nights later to check their tire pressure, park he did. "Don't mind the semis, Hardy Boy," she'd told him. "I'm sure they'll see you." So tonight's request—that he drive to the Zip-In

for a pint of Jack and a scratch-off lotto ticket—
came with some relief. Easiest thing he'd done
all week, for true.

A few minutes to seven, Hardy arrived at
the liquor store and parked next to a black late-
model truck splashed with mud. He got out and
admired the Chevy's lines. If he had a truck like
that, he'd polish it to a high shine and never,
ever get it dirty. Hell, if he had a truck like that,
he'd drive it all the way to Houma, maybe even
tonight, trading the swamp of Houston for the
swamp of his youth. But Hardy had an Impala,
his wife's Impala, a car that broke down every
time the wind blew. And since she'd sold his
Buick last week to pay for a new back brace, he'd
have to go without wheels of his own until the
sheetrocking business picked up again.

When he entered the store, he caught
himself on the closed-circuit monitor over the
door. His bald spot glinted in the fluorescent
light. The size of a gator egg, the hairless patch
may as well have been the size of an ostrich egg
the way Vera carried on about it, always holding
up a mirror to let him see. He'd thought about
holding one up to her backside until he realized

it would take a mirror the size of Terrebonne Parish to catch her fat ass. He waved to Aziz behind the safety glass and headed for the whiskey aisle. Aziz waved back and flipped another page of his schoolbook. The kid's dad was a real *bon rien*, one of those turban guys, always shouting and pointing. But Aziz was okay.

Only two other customers occupied the Zip-In: the owners of the muddy truck. They stood near the end cap, next to a Jack Daniels Halloween display. Someone—Aziz, most likely—had taped construction paper bats and pumpkins to the shelf. One of the Chevy owners, a teenager with a gut and a trucker hat, held up two flasks for comparison. The other, a middle-aged guy with thick black hair and leathery skin, idled a few feet away, hands in his pockets. Both wore sun-bleached Wranglers.

Hardy reached past them to grab his own bottle. If he hurried, he'd still make it home for the last half of the LSU game on ESPN. The Tigers were making jamma outta 'Bama.

"You a friend of Jack, too?" the middle-aged guy asked him. He had one of those rodeo belt buckles, looked like a silver dinner plate.

"Guess I am," Hardy said. "When I'm not palling around with Johnnie or Jim."

The man snickered and elbowed his young friend. "Hear that, Wade? We found us a whiskey expert, right here on West Bellfort. That's luck, isn't it?"

"I reckon so, Uncle Jerry." Wade looked at Hardy, eyes shadowed by the brim of his hat. "Which do you think I should buy, mister?" He offered up his bottles.

Hardy set his own Jack back on the shelf, donned the bifocals he kept clipped to his shirt, and took Wade's liquor. With those chubby cheeks and soft, flat hair of his, the kid couldn't have been more than eighteen, but Hardy wasn't much on meddling. He'd been a dumb kid once, too. Had to be to marry Vera. "Either one will paddle your *pirogue*, son, but the trip'll be smoother with this here." He held up the hooch with the silver label. "It's what I'd buy if I had the money."

"What about the black label?" Jerry asked.

"That Jack's a killer, too. All depends on your hurry." Hardy winked at the older man. "That what you are, son? In a hurry?" he asked Wade.

"It's not for me, it's for—"

Jerry laid a hand on his nephew's shoulder. "We said it was secret, didn't we, boy?"

Hardy propped his bifocals on his head. LSU could wait. "*What* was secret?"

Jerry craned his neck around a Captain Morgan cutout and looked at Aziz. Aziz hadn't moved from the cashier's booth. "Our trip to the Piney Woods," he said to Hardy.

"I'm sure we can trust him, Uncle Jerry," Wade said. "Don't you reckon?"

Jerry studied Hardy. Hardy let him. Hardy hadn't noticed before, but Jerry wore a gold Rolex. This man had secrets, and Hardy wanted to know them. All his life he'd wanted to know them. But nobody in the Thibault family had ever figured their way to a Rolex, except for Cousin Floyd, and he'd had to trade his for an orange jumpsuit. Sticking around also beat going home and watching Vera get loaded.

After a minute, Jerry nodded to Wade, and Wade said, "We're going Jack hunting."

"Jack hunting?" Hardy raised his eyebrows. "You mean hunting drunk? Like with Jack Daniels?"

"No," Wade said. "*Jack*alope hunting."

Hardy chuckled. That was Houston for you. "Good luck with that." He reached for Vera's whiskey again. He might catch the rest of the LSU game after all.

"You don't believe us, mister?" Wade said.

"Don't let that stop you," Hardy said. "Don't believe in church, either, but people keep right on praying." He touched his own watch, a Timex, and righted it on his wrist. "Just tell me one thing. What's with the whiskey?"

Wade lowered his voice. "It's the critters' favorite drink. Calls them from the woods every time. When they come into the open, we hit 'em—BLAM!—right between the eyes." He settled on the black label, trading the flask for the big bottle.

"The four-pointers go for a thousand, and the six-pointers..." Jerry rubbed his mouth. His watch glinted. "The six-pointers go for ten grand, easy. But the older they get, the craftier they get. Usually takes three to bag them: one to ambush and two to shoot. You could join us. We'd all get rich."

Hardy crossed his arms. "You think I'm some *couyon*, fresh from the bayou?"

"Suit yourself," Jerry said. "Let's go, Wade."

Hardy watched the two cowboys approach Aziz's glass box. The younger man set the whiskey on the counter, along with a bag of pork skins and a packet of pickle salt. The older man took a fistful of money from his pocket, peeled off a bill, and shoved it through the pay hole. Aziz's eyes brightened at the wad of cash. Hardy sucked the last bit of pot roast from his back teeth. He knew jackalopes didn't exist. But if they didn't, how did Jerry come by that watch? And that Chevy? All sorts of critters could be hiding in Texas, he reasoned, even make-believe ones. Even *he* believed in the *rougarou*, the beast of the bayou.

"Tee-Hardy," Maw Maw said to him when he was nine, "don't go breaking lent or the *rougarou* will have you for dinner." Since Hardy always did as he was told, he buried his Paydays in his underwear drawer, saving them for over a month until he gave in to temptation, risking damnation for a peanut bar—three of them to be exact, eaten the Saturday before Easter. On the way to St. Frances de Sales the next morning, the shadow of the *rougarou* scrambled behind him and latched onto him with its cold claws. Up to then, he'd thought the Cajun werewolf a legend, a figment to make kids behave; up to then, he hadn't traded his eternal soul for a nougat log. The creature haunted him for weeks, never materializing in the flesh, always appearing in ragged silhouette, as if ripped from the black cloth of Father Poitou's cassock, until Hardy swore off his beloved candy. You might catch him with the occasional Zagnut, but his Paydays were behind him.

Jackalopes weren't much of a stretch, all things considered. And then there was the money.

"Wait!" Hardy called to the cowboys. "Wait for me!"

It took about an hour for Jerry to drive them to Willis and meander down the small farm-to-market road toward the Sam Houston National Forest. In that time, the sun had set. Hardy rubbed his legs, cramped from sitting sideways in the truck's tiny back seat. Jerry rolled down the windows and let in a blast of cold air that whipped Hardy's hair around his bald spot. The two men had been plenty talkative back in Houston, but the farther they drove from town, the quieter they got. Doublewides ticked off the miles until they turned into the forest.

The truck hit a bump, and Hardy knocked his head against the shotgun rack. Right now, his wife was probably sitting in her recliner, cursing him for dawdling. He smiled. After tonight's score, he'd downshift from Vera Time to Houma Time. Her voice grated his memory: "Hurry now, Hard Boy! Step and fetch it!" He couldn't wait to leave her fat ass. She hadn't always been a nag. But like the *rougarou*, she'd undergone a change these last twenty-two years, transforming into a grotesque shadow of her former self that clung to him as much as any

Cajun werewolf. Hardy shuddered and rubbed away the *frissons*. The nightmares of his childhood hadn't disappeared; he'd learned to live with them.

The city lights of Willis, if you could call them that, had all but disappeared behind the thick pines that towered on either side of the road. Moths streaked across the windshield, drawn by the headlamps. The light comforted Hardy. Jerry's hi-beams cut through the dark like the prow of a ship, parting a blackness he hadn't seen since Houma in the seventies. Now, Chili's and Wal-Mart tainted the night sky of his hometown, turning it a dull brown. That was progress for you.

"We almost there?" he asked.

"Almost," Wade said. He held the whiskey bottle between his legs. The neck stuck straight up like a glass *bibitte*.

Jerry lifted his phone from the cup holder, thumbed through his texts, and dropped it back. His charm had worn off, but the glint of his Rolex hadn't. Would Hardy's share of ten grand pay for a watch like that? It might, if he spent the whole thing on it. No, Hardy Boy, he reminded himself, you're going to spend yours on living. A single man can do a lot with a little in Houma if he doesn't squander it first. Hardy's bladder twinged as the truck pulled into a gravel turnaround and parked. He'd been holding his water since Conroe.

Jerry killed the engine, but kept the battery on to power the headlights. Then he and Wade climbed out and stretched their arms overhead.

"We all gettin' down?" Hardy asked from the backseat.

"Gettin' down where?" Wade asked.

"Never mind," Hardy said. He reached around and flipped the lever, sending the front seat forward. He stepped to the gravel and stretched his legs. Any other Thibault would've balked at a trip to the woods with armed strangers. Not Hardy. And for this, he would be the first Thibault to get rich. A moth flew past him and dove for the headlamp, crashing against the hi-impact plastic. Hardy snickered at the insect's stupidity, then turned to Jerry. "Where we at?" he asked him.

"Middle of nowhere," he said. "Let's grab our guns, Wade."

While the men unhooked their weapons from the gun rack, Hardy picked a tree to pee behind. When he unzipped, Jerry withdrew from the truck and shouted at him the way Aziz's dad shouted at Aziz, like he'd spilled gunpowder in the gumbo.

"What the hell are you doing?" he snapped at Hardy. "You want to ruin the hunt with your scent?"

"*Mais, no.*" Hardy zipped up and hustled back to the men. "Guess it can wait."

Jerry took his 12 gauge from Wade and opened the action to check the cartridges, then he clacked it shut. "You ready to make some money?" he asked his nephew.

"Sure am," Wade said. Red crept across his chubby cheeks.

"Me, too," Hardy added.

Jerry reached through the open truck window and turned the key, cutting the juice to the battery. The headlamps clicked off. Night flooded the turnaround.

"What's the plan?" Hardy asked. He counted to ten in French to take his mind off his bladder. *Une, deux, trois...*

"You walk ahead," Jerry said to him, "and flush one out. Wade and I will come behind you and shoot." Jerry's phone vibrated. He pulled it from his pocket and thumbed in a reply. The glow of the screen washed his arm in blue.

"How will I know when I find a jackalope?" Hardy asked.

"I reckon you'll know," Wade said. "Can't miss the antlers." He rested the shotgun casually over one shoulder. "It's this way, right Uncle Jerry?" He nodded to a part in the woods.

"So it is," Jerry said. He clapped Hardy on the shoulder and looked him in the eye. "You go ahead. Don't be afraid now. Just keep walking. We'll be along soon enough."

Hardy took a step and paused. "We forgot the whiskey."

"We did, didn't we?" Jerry sneered at his nephew. "Wade, pull your head out of your ass and get the whiskey for me."

Wade hustled to the truck, belly bouncing, and retrieved the alcohol. He handed it to Jerry who handed it to Hardy. "You're an asset, Hardy Boy," Jerry said to him. "A real *ass-et.*"

Hardy thanked him and headed down the narrow trail like he'd been told. Trees filtered what little light the crescent moon spilled on him, making the forest even darker than the turnaround. Hardy liked being an asset. He'd never been one before. No Thibault ever had, to Vera's reckoning. He'd gone twenty or thirty yards when the stitch in his groin began to unravel in the most painful way. Surely Jerry would understand his need for a detour. Hardy cut between two saplings and unzipped a second time.

"You see anything?" Jerry called to him. He sounded farther back on the trail, but still too close for Hardy's liking.

"No, not yet," Hardy replied. He left the trail, pushing deeper into the woods so Jerry wouldn't yell at him again. Boat shoes, to no one's surprise and least of all his own, weren't the best choice for hiking. He stumbled over three fallen logs before finding a man-made clearing dotted with stumps. He tucked the bottle of Jack under his arm and whizzed on the bark of the tallest pine to see if he could knock a piece off. Thin moonlight shone on the trunk, revealing a set of tiny scratches near the base of the tree. If Hardy hadn't known better, he would've sworn an itty-bitty buck made them. It *was* late October and close to rut season, but the size of the marks surprised him.

After zipping his fly, Hardy cracked the bottle seal and took a swig of the black label. The whiskey swept away the woolies, letting him think clearly for the first time since the Zip-In. Something Jerry said bothered him, but he didn't know what. He rifled through the tackle box in his head and found with two words: Hardy Boy. "You're a real asset, Hardy Boy," the cowboy had said. How did Jerry know his nickname? Had he mentioned it to the men on the ride over? He didn't think so. Then how did Jerry—

A stick cracked.

Just a *chaoui*—a raccoon—he told himself. He took another swig. Jerry and Wade had cozied up to him pretty quick at the liquor store. Maybe too quick. His stomach gurgled when he recalled Jerry's words: "Middle of nowhere. Grab our guns." He might not be the first Thibault to make it big after all.

"Hardy Boy?" Jerry's voice rang through the trees. "Come out, come out, wherever you are. We've got some hunting to do."

Hardy's hand trembled, churning the whiskey in the bottle. He took another swig to calm his nerves. A bush rustled, frazzling them again. He strained to see through the thick greenery, expecting the cowboys to leap into the clearing, bear-cutters aimed at his chest. When they didn't, he lowered his gaze, letting it come to rest on a jackrabbit near the edge of the clearing. Small and brownish, it had spindly legs, spoon-shaped ears, and the finest rack Hardy had ever seen on a hare. *Mais, no*, the *only* rack Hardy had ever seen on a hare. Hardy rubbed his eyes and looked again to be sure.

It was the jackalope, for true.

Hardy shook the bottle of whiskey and chuckled. The scent had called the critter from the woods like Wade promised. He and Jerry had been telling the truth after all. He counted the points on the jackalope's battle-scarred antlers. "One, two, three, four…" He grinned. "Six! Six points!" He dribbled some whiskey on the ground, calling the *petite lapin* closer. It drank the liquor with more gusto than Vera on a Saturday night. "Jerry! Wade! I found him!" he shouted.

Jerry and Wade hollered back and forth on the trail, their voices indistinct. "Where'd he go?" one asked. "Thought you knew!" the other replied. Then some cussing and whatnot. Hardy chuckled. They'd pass by soon enough. When he turned around, the jackalope looked a few inches bigger. He scratched his bald spot. Couldn't be.

Anxious from the men's shouting, the *petite lapin* bolted upright and wiggled its nose, delicate forepaws crossed in front of its white belly. Cutest thing Hardy had ever seen, cuter than the itty-bitty gator he found the summer he turned six. He looked into the fur ball's dewy brown eyes, and as he did, the fortune he'd dreamt about faded, replaced by an overwhelming urge to protect the animal; the creature's power was that strong. He dropped to one knee and cooed, "Aw, *cher bébé*, it's okay. I'll keep you safe from those bad old cowboys."

The jackalope sniffed the bottle in Hardy's hand.

"You still thirsty?" Hardy poured more liquor on the ground—a cup at least—saving the rest for himself. He would need it after tonight.

The jackalope lapped the amber liquid, transforming before Hardy's eyes. As it drank, the *petite lapin* became the *lapin*, which gave way to the *grosse lapin*. The creature grew bigger…and bigger…and bigger with each sip of eighty proof. Pines cracked and bent with the expansion of its hind end. When the puddle ran dry, the beast rose to its full height, knocking timber sideways with a frame so gigantic, so frightening, it made the *rougarou* look like the suckling kitten of the bayou. Hardy dropped to his knees and covered his head to fend off falling branches. Once the last of them hit the ground, he peeked through his arms.

Forty, fifty feet tall, the jackalope towered above Hardy, its antlers reaching for the tree line. *If* Hardy survived this ordeal, he'd return to

Houma, with or without money. Hell, he'd walk to Louisiana if he had to; Texas was too dangerous. The monstrous hare studied him with eyes the size of basketballs. Hardy's breath came hard and fast. To keep from becoming a Cajun toothpick, he warbled a lullaby Maw Maw used to sing about a *poulette* laying eggs on the moon. The jackalope laid its ears back, calmed by the whiskey and the music. But when Jerry and Wade crashed into the clearing, those ears shot forward again. The monster roared, shaking needles from the pines and blasting Wade's hat from his head.

"Holy shit!" Wade shouted. "It's real, Uncle Jerry! The jackalope's real!" His shotgun pointed toward the ground. In all the excitement, he'd forgotten to lift his weapon.

Not Jerry. He leveled his 12 gauge at the jackalope's heart.

The monster flashed its long, yellow teeth and thumped the ground in warning. The force of its back leg rumbled the earth, rattling fallen branches and scattering loose dirt. Jerry kept his footing and put his finger on the trigger, cool as a *caimon*.

"No!" Hardy shouted. He jumped to his feet and dove for the cowboy, but like all Thibault men before him, Hardy came up short.

The jackalope, however, did not.

The monster swooped down and bit Jerry clean in two, right at the beltline, with incisors the length of a man's arm. Jerry's business end—the end inside the jackalope's mouth—let loose with a wet, blood-soaked scream that trailed off as it slid down that enormous gullet. The man never fired a shot.

"Uncle Jerry!" Wade shrieked.

Hardy turned and retched at the spectacle of Jerry's leftovers. Muscles locked in place, the cowboy's bottom half stood at the ready, waiting for the return of its top half. Seconds later, a red waterfall spilled over the big silver belt buckle, and the legs crumpled to the ground, crotch first. Hardy puked again—*oo ye yi*, the whiskey burned—and clutched the earth to keep from doubling with fright. He wanted to sprint to the truck and lock himself inside, but his legs felt about as useful as Jerry's. He fell back on his ass in time to see Wade lift his gun.

The kid shouldered his weapon, hands shaking.

Hardy bit his knuckles and waited for the obvious outcome. From the sweat on Wade's upper lip and the wet streak moving down his pants leg, he knew the obvious outcome, too. And the jackalope did not disappoint. The creature lowered its head and charged, impaling Jerry's nephew against the trunk of a pine tree with four of his six points. The kid coughed and sputtered for Hardy's help with lungs obviously punctured. "Hhhhhhardee," he wheezed. "Hhhhhhardeeeeee…"

Hardy thought about grabbing the nearby shotgun, but decided against it. A fat, middle-aged Cajun with a bald spot was no match for the Terror of the Piney Woods, even with a 12 gauge. The jackalope withdrew and let its victim sink to the ground. Overcome with fright, Wade thrashed on the forest floor as he tried to right himself and crawl away. The movement must have angered the horned hare from hell. Or excited it. The jackalope grasped the kid with its long, yellow teeth and lifted him in the air.

Hardy covered his face and winced at the horrible sounds that followed. Grinding. Crunching. Ripping. Chewing. He bargained with God to let him live; he begged God to let him live. When silence crept back to the woods, Hardy withdrew his hands and squinted into the dark. Only Wade's trucker hat and rifle remained. The items lay next to Jerry's legs in a gruesome lost and found pile. The monstrous killer had disappeared, too, replaced by the loveable, dark-eyed snippet of fur again. After satisfying its appetite, the jackalope had shrunk to normal size. It sat a few feet from Hardy, cleaning its paws and face of blood.

"There's a good *bébé*," Hardy said to the creature. He crawled to the whiskey bottle and screwed the top on tight to prevent another growth spurt. The beast had already indulged in an appetizer and main course. Hardy didn't fancy himself dessert.

The jackalope finished grooming itself, missing a tiny droplet of red on the end of its whisker—the only thing awry on an otherwise meek jackrabbit. It glanced at Hardy with a look akin to gratitude, then hopped to a nearby tree trunk to sharpen its antlers, the same trunk Hardy had whizzed on before.

Once he'd caught his breath, Hardy cleared the scene of evidence, starting with Wade's belongings. He kicked the kid's gun and hat under a cluster of shrubs and covered them with fallen branches for good measure. If anyone found them, they'd think Hardy had something to do with the teen's disappearance. And didn't he? He'd been tonight's bartender, after all. Grunting with exertion, he dragged Jerry's lower half toward those same bushes, leaving a maroon trail that glinted in the dark.

The cowboy's pants vibrated, alerting Hardy to an incoming text.

Winded, he let the legs drop and emptied the man's pockets—something he should've done before had he not been praying so hard. He took out the wad of cash, the truck keys, and the vibrating cell. These were his now. "Too bad you swallowed the Rolex," he said to the hare. "I could've used that." He turned his attention to the phone and thumbed through the texts.

Jerry's last outgoing message: *lost your boy in woods*.

The newest incoming message: *find him and kill him*.

The texter? Vera.

"Son of a bitch," Hardy said. The cash, the hunting invitation, Jerry's mention of "Hardy Boy," and Vera's late night request for whiskey—they all added up to murder for hire. He thumbed through the bills and counted eighteen hundred dollars. Two grand for the Buick minus two hundred for the back brace equaled one bullet through his head. He shoved the money in his pocket. If anyone should've have hired a hit man, it should've been him. Vera was the human equivalent of flypaper: the more he struggled against her, the harder she stuck to him. Now she'd paid someone to kill him, swat him like a fly and leave his body to the ants.

Hardy scratched his bald spot and studied the jackalope, letting a plan float to the surface. A minute later, he texted Vera: *it's done, Hardy Boy is gone*. Then he shook the bottle and sloshed the liquor, luring the creature. "Come along, Jacque, come along. We've got some drinking to do."

Using the whiskey as bait, Hardy led his new pet all the way to Jerry's truck, correction, *his* truck. Navigating the back roads took some time, but once he turned onto I-45 and hit eighty miles an hour, the city skyline materialized in no time. If everything happened as planned, he and Jacque would be tucked into a plate of boudin and rice by noon tomorrow. Hardy could almost smell the brackish waters of Lake Boudreaux from here.

On the outskirts of Houston, Hardy passed by a carwash and scrubbed the mud from his new Chevy, returning it to factory black. With that done, he continued toward town. For most of the ride, Jacque looked out the passenger window. But when they exited onto Loop 610, Hardy's pet grew more and more restless, thumping its back leg and turning circles on the bucket seat. He stroked its ears and spoke in a soft voice, "Go *do-do*, little one. Go to sleep." That didn't work, so he hummed Maw Maw's lullaby all the way to West Bellfort. It settled the jackalope some, but not enough for Hardy's liking. When they hit the cracked driveway of the Zip-In, Jacque let out a large belch, depositing the Rolex on the seat.

Hardy wiped the timepiece on his pants and snapped it onto his wrist. "Bet you feel better now." He laughed. "I know I do."

Jacque nudged Hardy's hand.

"Don't worry. I'll be back, little fella," Hardy whispered as he got down from the truck. "You stay here and work up a thirst."

At first, Aziz refused to let him in the store—ten after nine, and the Zip-In had closed—but he changed his mind when Hardy pulled a hundred from his pocket and stuck it against the window. The Cajun grinned as he passed under the close-circuit cameras. A man could do a lot with a little, even in Houston, Texas. But he'd already set his heart on Houma. He and Jacque would be there by daylight, and nothing could stop him.

Then, because Hardy always did as he was told, he bought a bottle of whiskey and a scratch-off lotto ticket before heading home to Vera.

Moments

Ellen Rothberg

IN THE SOUTHEAST PART of Texas, autumn rumbles in between Halloween and Thanksgiving. People start pulling out sweaters because the first glimpse of leaves falling off the trees or the moment a wind turns in an unexpected direction with even a hint of coolness is cause to celebrate. And folks don't waste even a minute that can be used to dress in anything but the summer clothing they've been wearing since March. It wasn't that kind of Monday, though. It was impossibly humid and the temperature was already past 80 in the early morning promising to darken the moods of summer weary Houstonians. By 6:00 A.M. the diehard joggers were heading down the paths all over town. They moved with just a hint of fatigue as they nodded knowingly to each other on the various paths dotting the city. In Montrose, with the cracking city sidewalks. In the Heights, amid the mass revitalizing of previously forgotten bungalows. In Memorial Park, where more joggers start their day than any other place in town. And, even in the suburbs, people laced up their running shoes and headed out, sweating before they even made it past their manicured lawns.

Some people can't let go of the never ending edginess that accompanies living in a place where the heat broils everything, mercilessly, making even getting in your car cause for an extra shower. But on this Monday, the staff at Rambling Creek Elementary School had even more cause for concern. The air conditioning had not kicked on from the weekend and the thermostat in the front office hovered at 79 degrees. *Not too bad*, one might be tempted to think, however, the seven hundred plus students were just beginning to arrive and the temperature outside was already rising.

Monday 7:35 A.M. Michelle

"It's a beautiful morning," I said cheerily to Tanya, the school's secretary. "It's a little warm in here, don't you think?"

"I know," said Tanya, fanning herself with a copy of the school lunch menu. "I have already called maintenance. They said we were fifth in line for a chiller check this morning. The good news is that the heat is keeping many of the parents from hanging around in the office."

True, the office was eerily empty. We worked hard at keeping the parents from prolonged good byes with their children. The unofficial rule was to keep all adults out until after the morning announcements were over, or until everyone had started their second cup of coffee.

"You already missed it, Michelle. Couldn't you get here just five minutes sooner?" Tanya smiled as she filled me in on the parent with the latest problem that had to absolutely be handled right that very minute. "She kept screaming, 'Where's the guidance counselor? Where's the guidance counselor?' I thought she was going to throw an embolism."

"Well, it's always a good sign if they don't know my name," I teased. "At least they won't come back with a gun looking for me."

We had joked about it, although it was never really a joking matter.

"Houston, we have a problem," Tanya said holding her right hand in the customary phone receiver pose. "Shooter in the building," she said. "Of course, I wouldn't be able to make that call because I'll be the first one to go." Tanya's face lost its previous cheeriness.

Our school, built before people went that kind of crazy, used to allow access without benefit of checking in, until the district remodeled encasing our entry in glass, complete with a buzzer system and a computerized management kiosk. The remodeling was part of a tax bond issue because everyone wanted to ensure school safety. Although the proposition had been passed several years before Sandy Hook, there was always a lag in accomplishing a remodel. The children in Connecticut had died right after our construction was completed. It was a hassle getting into our building now and we liked it that way, but Tanya was still out in the open in a glass box of an office. I patted Tanya lightly on the back, as I poured my second cup of coffee. We had the same conversation every few days. We laughed nervously because it could never happen to us. Not our school. Not our kids. Not our parents. Even our semi-crazy parents. Not us. I grabbed my coffee cup and walked to my office.

Monday 7:15 A.M. Randy

It felt like a Saturday. He should have been able to turn over and go back to sleep, but he was on the tens in the Houston Police Department. Ten days on and four days off. Two more days to go and he would take the kids for the four day break. Maybe he would keep them out of school for two days and go to the hill country. The kids would love it. Crystal would hate it. He could already imagine the conversation.

"I'm taking the kids to Kerrville for a couple of days," he'd say when he picked them up from the house that used to be his home, too.

"Oh no, you're not," he imagined Crystal arguing back. "If I call school and they're not there, I'm calling the police."

"I am the police, you idiot." Of course, he would leave out the name calling because he would never do that in front of the children. His children, his babies, torn away from him in the divorce. He was a good father. He was never late with child support even though Crystal made more money than him. He wanted to do the right thing by and for his children. He missed them. He missed being a family. Crystal wanted the divorce. He still didn't really understand why, but he was over losing Crystal, his high school sweetheart. Her words still rang in his ears.

"It's over, Randy. I'm so tired of your control over me. I want you out."

He couldn't stand losing his kids. He worried constantly about their well-being. He and Crystal had even met with Michelle Brinley, Rambling Creek Elementary's guidance counselor, to make sure they were doing everything they could to help them adjust.

"Kids are fairly resilient. Your attitudes and behavior will either strengthen or weaken their ability to cope. If you treat each other with respect and present a unified front as far as Danny and Maddie are concerned, they should be fine," Michelle had said, "And, of course, make sure that you let them know the divorce is not their fault." Danny was seven when they divorced. He had a rough time, but his talks with Michelle had provided an outlet during the school day enabling him to blow off some much needed steam before his academics began to suffer. Now nine, he was a good, well-adjusted student.

The joint custody agreement, on the other hand, was exhausting. There were constant threats from his ex-wife about taking the kids to live in Austin so she could be closer to the boyfriend that helped break up their marriage. Pride and fear kept him from agreeing to the move. He still owed the lawyer money and every time he had to go to court to keep her from leaving Houston, added another chunk of money to what he owed.

The shower pulsed hot water over his body. Two more days and Detective Randall Conley could spend some quality time with his kids. He hoped it would be a quiet Monday in Houston.

Monday 10:10 A.M. Michelle

When I heard the three shots, I knew. I didn't have to see her. I just knew. The parent desperately wanting to see me was in the building with a gun. It was just that simple. It happened in the blink of an eye. I heard the shots and walked quickly to my door. I closed it, calmly, silently. The instant connection of cylinders slipping smoothly into place reminded me that the doors were always locked, always ready. I quickly flipped the light switch, plunging the office into almost total darkness. The window in the office door allowed light to filter in from the hallway, but just enough to slightly illuminate the furniture. I dove under the desk as the principal's voice broke through the silence over the PA system, with simple words and a slight tremor she said, "Lockdown, this is not a drill." More shots broke the silence coming from the front office. Fear spread through my body, starting in my chest and flowing out toward my head and feet in waves. Before today, I had always wondered what went through someone's mind when they were facing what could be their last moment in this world. Now I knew. I prayed silently to a God I hadn't really thought about for a long time and wondered who had entered the school.

My eyes were still adjusting to the darkness when I heard her voice.

"Where is that bitch counselor? Get out of my way," her voice both shrill and inhuman, transported me back to our last conversation, just two weeks before.

"You told me my child would meet with you every day," Ms. Taylor whined.

"I never said every day, Ms. Taylor. I said we could meet as time allowed," I explained, "I can't pull your child out of class for hours at a time, as much as I would like to be able to meet her need to leave her room." The last part thrown in to validate the concerns the parent had for her first grader, who absolutely refused to stay in her classroom for longer than fifteen minutes at a time.

"You're a liar," she pointed her finger at me from across the table in our little conference room. "You don't care about my baby at all," she moaned. "No one will help us, what are we going to do, my baby needs help!"

The "baby" in question had run away from home half a dozen times, had shown up at school bruised and bleeding and had recently disclosed details which prompted me to take action. Evidence pointed at abuse by her mother. I had reported it to Child Protective Services, confidentially, of course, and they investigated, but no formal charges had been filed and I felt judged by mom who, no doubt, believed I was the whistle-blower to CPS.

"Ms. Taylor, you know you can call the support services I provided you with last week," wearily I looked through my file for the therapist's card. "I am not a psychotherapist and I can't provide you and your daughter with the care you need. It is outside my scope of therapy."

"Therapy? Therapy? You can't provide us with therapy? Well, what do you do around here anyway?" Ms. Taylor slammed the door on her way out.

At the time, I had planned to call a therapist friend to see if she could help Ms. Taylor and her daughter, Ellie. Knowing a follow-up call was necessary, I even wrote it in my calendar. Time got away from me, though. There were always so many things for me to do. Of course, I now realized I had never made the call to my therapist friend and I had never tried to call Ms. Taylor either. Marnie Taylor had been the parent who needed to see me so badly early that morning. And because of me, she was shooting up the front office of Rambling Creek Elementary on a sultry fall day. A day that would now become front page news all over the country. A day, when seven hundred plus students and their teachers would be stuck interminably in their classrooms with no air conditioning, frightened by the words their principal had uttered. Words that were followed by gun shots and silence.

Sunday 9:46 P.M. Marnie

find the backpacks, get the papers signed. what did they need, what did they need? where did

i put the folders? why was there always so much paperwork? why were they always asking me

to sign things? why couldn't the damn school keep all the papers there? i could get these papers and sign them when it's really necessary. these papers are bullshit.

"Kyle, Kyle where is your school folder," she screamed from the foyer. No answer.

"Kyle!" She ran to his room. "Kyle, wake up! We have to find the folder," she shook him by the shoulder, but he didn't move.

crap, crap see what you did, counselor, see what happens when you make people think i'm a bad mother?

He was so still, she had to look at him really closely. She remembered him as a baby. All chubby and cuddly. They were happy then, she and Carl and baby Kyle.

"Mommy?" Ellie's voice from the other room.

shit, now she's awake and I'll have to deal with her.
Marnie wrung her hands fretting about whether
or not she had taken her meds. *was it today? did i
take them this morning or was it the day before?*

Monday 10:20 A.M. Randy

    The line was really long. He hated that. It
tested his patience. He thought about pulling his
badge out and breaking the line, but decided
against it. He thought about all of the money he
spent on coffee. He was going to have to start
brewing his coffee at home or switch to the
regular coffee of the day. He couldn't afford to
spend $25 a week on designer coffee. He looked
at his watch. Since the divorce, he couldn't
afford to spend much money on anything.
Running two households was depleting his
funds rapidly. He sighed. The line was moving
so slowly this morning. His phone rang. He was
surprised to see the caller I.D. flash Crystal's
number. She rarely called him unless she wanted
to complain about something he either did or
didn't do as it related to Danny and Maddie. He

knew he wasn't late with the child support payment, so reluctantly, he answered the call.

"Yeah," Randy said impatiently.

"Randy," Crystal sounded worried, "I think something's going on at school. Maddie forgot her lunch, and I stopped here on my way to work to drop it off. There are several police cars here and they aren't letting anyone in."

"What the hell?" Randy broke out of the coffee line and covered his left ear with his hand to better hear what Crystal was saying. At the same time, an emergency call broke in from his precinct.

"Crystal, hold on, I'm getting a call from the precinct dispatch," he hit call waiting, "Conley," he listened intently and then switched back to Crystal, "I'm on my way to the school." Randy broke into a run as he left Starbucks.

He didn't wait for his latte.

As he sped out of the Starbucks parking lot, He reached for the button on the dash to turn on his sirens.

Monday 10:15 A.M. Michelle

The kindergarteners would be getting hungry. It was their lunchtime. I didn't know why that struck me when I had other things to worry about, like getting killed. Maybe because I glanced at my watch out of habit. The tiny diamond chips glowed in the backlit face of the watch, a gift from Matt on my last birthday. My last birthday. That had new meaning now. My knee brushed against my purse, thrown thoughtlessly every morning under the desk. How many times had my assistant Courtney warned me about putting it in the closet?

"You're too trusting, Michelle," she warned, "You never know who's going to come by and help themselves to whatever you have in there."

Where is Courtney, I wondered as I fumbled to find my cell phone. In crisis training, we were told to stay off our cell phones. I never could figure out how the outside world was going to know what was happening if we didn't call out. I didn't care what the protocol was, I turned the ringer off and texted my husband.

Emergency shooter in the school lockdown
help

I thought for a second and added:

I love you take care of kids

A tear slid down my cheek and I hurriedly wiped it away and pressed send. I will not think about my children now. I will not think about my poor children and what they would do without me. My children need me. I will not die here. Not today.

Frozen. Time really did stand still. My joints ached. I was drenched in sweat. I glanced at my watch again. 10:18.

I heard a voice in the hallway. Someone was coming down the corridor outside my office. I held my breath and scrunched deeper under the desk, grateful for the thick wood that protected me from instant detection should the door to the office open. But, it's locked. I remembered that we have been told to keep it locked at all times. I remembered to breathe.

Funny, such a natural body function can be forgotten in times of panic.

Monday 10:10 A.M. Marnie

 stupid people, stupid people. always in my way. they know me, why do i have to sign in and get a stupid pass with my picture on it. i just need to find that counselor.

"Where is she, get her up here, now!" she screamed.

 stupid people, stupid people. just get out of my way and you won't get hurt. don't make me use this. you just can't stop stupid. but i know how to stop stupid. just like i stopped stupid at home with the kids. why can't they ever just answer a question when i ask it?

Monday 10:25 A.M. Randy

 Arriving on the scene did nothing to quell his fear. It was pandemonium. He quickly found someone in uniform, a school district officer named O'Malley. He didn't tell the young officer that his children attended the school and were, no doubt, hunkered down in their classrooms. He pushed the thought from his mind.

"I'm Detective Conley, HPD. Are the local police here? What about HPD, have they been called in?

"We received several calls, the official one came through the district police after a silent alarm came over their emergency line," Officer O'Malley said. He was very young and this was his first major assignment. Randy thought he looked a little green and he tried to calm him down as he struggled into the bulletproof vest he kept in his car.

"Has Houston been called in?" he asked again quietly.

"Yes, S.W.A.T. should be here in less than five minutes," he replied, clearly on edge from his assignment as information officer.

"Good work," Randy replied tapping him gently on the shoulder, "I'm going in."

"No, you can't. I'm under strict orders not to allow breaching of the building until plenty of back-up has arrived," O'Malley objected.

Randy thought for several seconds and looked O'Malley in the eye. He knew Houston S.W.A.T. would take over when they arrived. He had no intention of waiting until they got there and started putting a plan together. He would control the situation.

"We can stand here and argue or you can give me that headset and let me get started on finding a way into the building that doesn't startle the shooter. Let me remind you that I'm a detective and, yes, I'm pulling rank. Now, see if you can get these people to back up," Randy adjusted the vacated headset. He didn't know who O'Malley was reporting to, but any connection to the outside would be better than none. He was about to take off for the rear of the school building when Crystal ran up.

"What's going on, Randy?" She was crying and her mascara was running down her cheeks.

"I'm going to find a way in," Randy said, "Make sure you tell HPD I'm in there and that I have a school district headset, OK. Don't worry." He added the last part because she looked so scared. Their babies were in the building.

Randy knew the school well. His children had attended since they were old enough for kindergarten. He helped coach the little league team whose players all attended school at Rambling Creek. He worked with Boy Scout Troop 782, Danny's group. Rambling Creek was his school.

Through his borrowed headset, he could hear the details   coming from the dispatch. He learned that one of the calls had come from the nurse's office. She had reported that the lone shooter was a parent screaming for the counselor. Randy knew the counselor fairly well. Michelle had been helpful in working with the kids during the divorce.

Randy hoped he could find a way into the building before S.W.A.T arrived and called him out for entering the building. He knew the custodial staff well and they did their best to keep the building locked up tight. He hoped his hunch would prove correct as he ran around to the trash dumpsters, heading for the backdoor. Sure enough he encountered one of the custodians he knew from his frequent lunches with Maddie.

"Mr. Johnson," Randy whispered, when he found the man crouched low behind the dumpster, "Do you have your keycard?" Mr. Johnson, Mr. J. to the kids he loved, was an institution at Rambling Creek.

"Officer Conley!" Mr. Johnson choked on the words, "I was putting out the trash when I heard the gunshots." He handed Randy his keycard.

"Stay here," Randy said, as he took the card and headed for the door to the custodian's office.

Randy assumed that the gunman was in the hallway behind the front office. If the perpetrator was in fact after the counselor, she would already be heading toward that office. Randy had not heard any shots coming from the building and he wondered why it would take so long to find the counselor. He pulled his gun from the holster and spoke briefly into his headset, hoping someone would respond on the other end.

"Entering the building from the custodian's office on the west side." Randy waited for a response.

"S.W.A.T. ETA is three minutes," O'Malley had secured another headset.

The keycard beeped quietly as he slipped through the door into the school. The quiet was eerie and Randy pushed back the fear that threatened his focus. Thinking about the safety of his own children at that particular moment would interfere with his ability to think fast, and he pushed the image of them out of his mind. Randy exited the custodian's office and crept quietly across the hallway so that he could edge closer to the office by flattening against the wall opposite the gymnasium. As he turned the corner, he could see the front office. The glass that had once surrounded the entrance was shattered. His view was obstructed by a pair of sofas that decorated the office space. As he inched his way closer, he could make out the forms of people, his breath caught, two children, their bodies partially covered by an adult, lay in a pool of blood. Randy stepped gingerly, quietly through the broken glass and around the bodies. As he made his way through the rubble, he took note of other bodies, but did not stop to check on them. He remained focused on his pursuit of the shooter. Randy turned the corner leading to the interior corridor and found himself behind the shooter. She obviously had no idea he was there. Marnie Taylor was ranting, but Randy could not make out what she was saying. The heat made him sweat even more in the bulletproof vest and he wondered if someone had turned off the air in the building.

Then, several things happened at once. Marnie Taylor fired three shots, shattering the glass inserts in Michelle's door. Randy couldn't make out what she was screaming, but whatever it was, it kept her focus away from him. He had to decide what to do. He pressed back against the wall to the principal's office. No more than twenty feet separated him from the intruder. At precisely the same moment, Houston police surrounded the building. A cell phone, Marnie's, began to ring. Marnie didn't answer. She was busy shooting up Michelle's office door.

"I know you're in there, bitch," she screeched, "Do you have time for me now?" Then, when she still could not open the office door, she jumped up, and perched for several seconds unsteadily on the frame of the broken window.

Randy raced down the hall, gun aimed and steady, he remembers that. Marnie was surprised, but turned and fired before falling backwards off the window frame into Michelle's office. He doesn't remember taking two slugs to the shoulder and upper chest. He fired at the same time, but was hit as his gun went off, the trajectory of the bullet veering off-course to Marnie's leg. He remembered thinking that it was a semi-automatic assault weapon, an odd choice for a woman. He heard one more shot and then blacked out.

Monday Michelle 10:35 A.M.

It was so quick. Afterwards, I couldn't believe how little time had passed. When I heard the exchange of gunfire, I stupidly looked out from behind the desk. I don't know why I did that. It goes against all the trainings I've had in what to do in an active shooter situation. I saw Marnie Taylor down on the ground, blood pouring from the wound in her thigh. Her gun waving dangerously in her limp hand. She tried to aim at me, but was already becoming woozy from the loss of blood. I could see someone, down in the hallway outside the office, not moving. I saw Marnie try to aim her gun at me. I was still on the floor and within reach of my purse. I opened it and withdrew the small-caliber pistol we were not permitted to have on campus. I stood and faced Marnie.

"I'm going to walk out of here now, Marnie. Put the gun down," I kept the gun on her as I slowly edged around the desk."

"You think you can get away with what you've done to my kids?" she asked, plainly having a difficult time trying to hold the gun on me.

"Put the gun down, Marnie, and we can talk about Kyle and Ellie," I said, never taking my eyes off her hand.

"I'm done talking," she said and tried to aim the gun.

"Me, too," I said and pulled the trigger.

Randy - Six Months Later

"Be careful, Danny, don't get too close to the edge." He smiled. It wasn't as if you could fall off a mountain in the Texas Hill Country. He took a deep breath. The air was clean and cool in the spring day. It felt good in his chest. He stretched his shoulder out. It still bothered him, especially in the damp weather which was pretty much all the time in Houston. He looked at his daughter, Maddie. She was getting so big, almost seven. He was thankful that Crystal had agreed to the little trip even though it meant taking the kids out of school. She was different after the shootings. He guessed they all were. They talked to each other more. Not so much at each other. Counseling provided by the school district helped them. They were even doing some things as a family. He smiled again. He had agreed to Crystal's move to Austin on a trial basis, but she said that she was reconsidering and would probably just stay in Houston after all.

He learned a few things about himself, too. He couldn't control everything all the time. While his superiors understood why he entered the building, he was suspended pending an investigation. In the end, he was exonerated from further disciplinary action, but it was clear that his cowboy actions would not be tolerated again.

"Daddy, why are you on a long vacation?" Maddie asked.

"Because I didn't listen and follow instructions from my boss," Randy had explained. "It's kind of like a time out."

"But you were just trying to keep us safe, right?" Maddie said, blue eyes imploring him to make sense of the whole mess.

"Maddie, sometimes it's necessary to break a rule, but there are always consequences even if you think you're making the right decision."

Maddie stopped asking about his suspension and began asking more questions about where her friends were now that they were dead. The twin girls killed along with their mother had been shot as they checked in late. One twin was a classmate. They had been to see the dentist.

And it was so hard to go back to Rambling Creek. It took months to repair the damage, so the students had been reassigned to neighboring schools. On their first day back, there was an extra moment of silence to honor the dead. Randy looked around the building as he dropped the kids off. He didn't want to leave them. He thought about his loss of control and how the therapist said he could try deep breathing to deal with his anxiety. He remembered his last conversation with Michelle.

"Where did you learn to shoot?" Randy asked. Michelle had come to visit him in the hospital.

"The range in Katy," she said.

"Is your gun registered?"

"Yes, Officer," she teased, "I have a license to carry a concealed weapon."

They laughed. It felt good to do something normal. Just as suddenly, they stopped laughing and a tear rolled down Michelle's cheek. People were gone, so normal was impossible to attain.

Michelle – Six Months Later

I just retired. Of course, that was after the school district suggested that it would be best if I did so. There was no way to explain why I was carrying a loaded weapon into the school building.

"It's against district policy, Mrs. Brinley," Ms. Porter, Director of HR said when I reported to the administration building following the incident. "An investigation has been ordered by the board."

Matt said we could hire an attorney to sort through the mess, but I just didn't have it in me. I guess I could have asked for Disability, Worker's Compensation claiming Post Traumatic Stress Disorder, but I just retired. I never stepped back into the school. The funerals were terrible, as funerals for massacre victims can be. Inexplicable tragedy, highlighting the horrific complications of mental illness provided fodder for network shows.

"Ms. Taylor suffered from Bipolar Disorder," reported channel 12 news, "It is believed at this time that she was not taking prescribed medications for the condition."

"The bodies of Taylor's children were found in their apartment just blocks from the school," reported Jack Nettles on CNN.

"Rambling Creek Elementary School Guidance Counselor, Michelle Brinley, has been hailed as a hero for her part in ending the standoff at the school. The gun used to kill Ms. Taylor was registered to Mrs. Brinley, but no information is available to explain why she had it at school. Mrs. Brinley was unavailable for comment," Fox News was relentless in their pursuit, but Matt refused their constant requests for an interview.

What would I tell them, anyway? I could say that as a counselor, I understand how difficult it is to treat someone who is not compliant about taking meds. Or maybe I could speak to the heartache I felt when I learned that Kyle and Ellie were dead. Certainly I could talk about the stages of grief and how processing them is imperative to closure. What stage of grief am I processing for the loss of Tanya, Courtney and our principal? And how do I explain the deaths of Cheryl Johnson and her seven-year-old twin girls who were signing in as late arrivals and just happened to be in the wrong place at the wrong time? And the gun? I have no answer for that either, but I had been carrying it in my purse for a year or so.

I don't wake up screaming as much as I did right after. Matt asks about the dreams all the time. I shake my head and say it doesn't matter what I'm dreaming about. They're just dreams. In the best dream, though, I call in sick on the day of the shootings and in the worst nightmare, the gun is in my hand and I am pulling the trigger.

Space City 6

In For A Penny

K.C. Maguire

*IF YOU SEE SOMETHING, SAY
SOMETHING*

The words mocked me from the poster taped to the wall of the faculty kitchenette. While it didn't specifically mention me, it may as well have. The details of the new university policy set out beneath the heading were searing as daylight.

> **"Assault will not be tolerated on
> this campus.** *Assault includes the*

puncturing of another's skin with any implement or body part (fingernails, teeth etc). The unauthorized ingestion of another's blood is strictly prohibited. It is an infringement of university policy and will result in disciplinary action. Consent by the victim is not a defense..."

Of course consent couldn't be a defense. Technically, people like me could glamour our prey, put them in our "thrall". Consent couldn't be meaningful in the legal sense. But the words still hurt. As if I'd ever do anything like that. I was prepared to expect this here. I remembered calling my mother when I first received the job offer.

"Mom, I finally got a position."
"That's great, Honey. Where?"
"Allen University."
"Houston?"
"Yeah."
"Did you check their recent diversity stats?"
"Yeah. I might have a problem."

The microwave beeped, and I retrieved the warm plastic packet, slicing the tab with a fingernail and pouring the viscous fluid into the waiting mug. I jammed the empty bag into the bottom of the trash and covered it with other refuse so no one would see it. Then I reached for the cup, plain and dark blue. I had picked it up at Wal-Mart precisely for this purpose, eschewing the novelty mug my best friend Sarah had given me as a congratulations gift when I took the job.

That one was deep red emblazoned with the image of a pair of fangs over the caption: "Vampires Do It in the Dark".

She said I should live up to who I was. What I was.

I didn't agree.

"Come on, Pens. They'll eat you alive if you don't stand up for yourself." Those had been her words when she helped me pack up my apartment so I could move into the college dorms. I wasn't required to live on campus, but it was the easiest choice to accommodate my schedule. My old apartment wasn't that far out of the city, but you could never bank on Houston traffic and I didn't want to get caught short, so it was safer to stay on campus.

"Ha. Very funny."

"I'm serious," she said. "You have to start being what you are. At least learn *how* to be what you are."

I grunted and turned back to the open drawer to shove the last of my belongings into the suitcase on the bed.

"Have you given any more thought to Vamps on Campus?" she asked. "I know you didn't join the chapter in grad school, but maybe now that you're going to be faculty?"

"Just stop, okay?" I silenced her with a wave of my hand, my nostrils flaring. I caught a hint of the distinctive coppery scent of her blood. "I don't need to sign up for a group to teach me how to bite people."

"It's not just learning how to stick your fangs into the good folk of Allen University." Sarah clutched at her neck in mock-horror. "They'd help you come to terms with who you are. Give you a sense of community. Teach you the skills you need to cope."

She pulled an object out of her jeans pocket.

My cellphone.

"What did you do?" I asked, cocking my head.

"Ugh, that's so creepy." She wrinkled her nose.

"What is?"

"That thing you do with your head. It's so … vamp-like."

I straightened my shoulders and grabbed for my phone, repeating the question. "What did you do, Sarah?"

"Nothing much. Just looked up the Vamps on Campus chapter at your new school and programmed their number in."

I shook my head and replaced the phone in my own pocket.

"You never know, Pens. You may need them."

"Not the Allen University bunch. They're probably a pack of vigilantes if that school's rep on diversity is anything to go by."

"All the more reason to have their number. They'll teach you how to stand up to those small-minded bigots."

I needed to change the tack of this conversation. I fingered the opal pendant around my neck, the one Sarah had always admired. I unsnapped the clasp and leaned over to press it into her hand.

"Oh no, Pens. I couldn't. It's your favorite."

"I want you to have it." I tightened my grip around her hand. She winced and I drew back. Occasionally, I still forgot my own strength.

"No." She opened her palm and raised it toward me. "It's too much like a goodbye. We'll still see each other all the time, right?" Tears welled in her eyes.

I couldn't let myself start to cry. It never bothered her, but I hated that my tears were pink now. "Then you can give it back to me next time we see each other. It will be on loan."

Her lip quirked in a half-smile. "Okay. Insurance that we'll keep in touch. I can buy that." She snapped the pendant around her neck.

If I was any other kind of friend, I would have offered to do it myself, but annoying as Sarah could be, I couldn't risk getting that close to her carotid.

After she left, I looked out my bedroom window, watching the stars twinkling in the clear sky. I hoped it was a good omen. I retrieved the phone from my pocket and scrolled through my contacts until I reached the "V"s. There it was. *Vamps on Campus – Allen University*. My finger hovered over the "Delete Contact" button for a moment, but I didn't press it.

Taking a hesitant sip from my mug, I felt the tension in my shoulders dissipate. I shouldn't have waited so long to feed, but I had some work to complete on a conference paper and had lost track of time. I was about to head back to my office but was distracted by the sound of two voices in the adjacent faculty library. Female colleagues. Sounded like Melanie Pike, a senior British History fellow, and Eleanor Glines, a professor specializing in Sumerian relics. I wouldn't have heard them without my heightened senses.

"*Did you hear who's going to be new department chair?*" Pike asked. "*Dawson.*"

"*What? No. That creep should be ineligible.*"

"*Because he married a student?*"

"*Yeah. Isn't that a breach of university policy?*"

"*Actually no. I checked.*"

"*That can't be right.*"

"*Hey, don't shoot the messenger. I'm just saying what I saw on the H.R. website.*"

"*Ugh. What time is it?*"

"*Six thirty.*"

"*I might head out then. Should have missed the bulk of the traffic by now.*"

"*You wish.*"

"*Right. No good time to get on to 59.*"

"*Drive safe.*"

A door clicked open and shut followed by silence. I took another sip from my mug. This time it didn't relax me at all. If Dawson was going to be the new department chair, that couldn't be good for me. I hadn't been here long, but long enough to know he wasn't particularly open-minded, except with respect to his own extra-curricular activities. I was going to have to fly under the radar for a while.

I glanced at my watch. It was actually closer to 6:45 and I had a class to teach at 7:00 P.M.

As usual, I checked my email the second I returned to my desk. There was only one new message. From my good friends in Human Resources.

> *"This is to advise that we will be unable to make the accommodation you requested for a mini-refrigerator and microwave in your faculty office. Building Services has advised that the power grid does not support such equipment in individual offices. Please do not hesitate to contact us if you have any queries. This file is now closed."*

My grip tightened around the computer mouse and I felt the plastic crack beneath my fingers. Tears welled in my eyes and I reached for a Kleenex to blot them. Human Resources had told me they didn't think the equipment in my office would be a problem. What would they do next? Cancel my night classes and make me teach in the middle of the day? The image of me bursting into flames at the podium came into my mind and I stifled a hysterical half-laugh, half-sob.

I shoved the pink-stained tissue into the bottom of the recycle bin beside my desk, under a sheaf of discarded draft pages of my conference paper.

"Excuse me?"

I started at the sound of the voice at my door. Why hadn't I bothered to close it? I looked up to see one of my students – Peter Thompson. Thomas? I had never been good with last names.

"Yes?" My voice sounded croaky and I struggled to steady it. "Can I help you with something?"

"Sorry, Prof, but I misplaced the reading assignment for tonight's class. Could you remind me what it was?" He took a step into the room, tall and tanned, wearing a pinstriped business suit. I noticed he had a cashmere scarf wrapped around his neck, completely hiding the skin underneath. Thankfully.

Night students were such a mixed bag. I wondered what his day job was.

"I posted it on the website, but," I said as I shuffled the papers on my desk, "I have it here too." I found what I was looking for and flicked to the relevant section. "Pages 50 to 70 of the prescribed text. On the early years of the Roosevelt administration."

"Teddy or F.D.?"

I raised an eyebrow. Okay, some of these students didn't pay much attention, but surely they knew whether or not they were enrolled in a class on the history of the Second World War.

"Chill, Prof. I'm only joking." A smile lit up his face, exposing shiny white teeth that looked like they may have been capped or at least polished to within an inch of their lives. His canines were perfectly rounded, unlike mine. "That your dinner?" He indicated the mug beside my computer monitor.

I stammered something in reply as he brushed a hand through his messy hair and tilted his head to the side, pushing his scarf down to expose the pulse-point at his neck. "Wouldn't you rather have the real thing?" The scent of copper immediately assaulted me, causing my mouth to water.

Vamp-fan! I'd come across his kind before but never in my class. Not yet at least. The ones who wanted to be bitten for the thrill of it.

My fangs elongated involuntarily. Desperately trying to ignore the sound of the blood pumping through his veins, I closed my eyes and forced myself to focus on pulling them back. "I think we should maybe get to class now, uh, Peter." The words came out slurred because my fangs weren't completely retracted.

"Sure thing, Prof. Or can I call you Penelope?" He winked as he raised his hand to replace the scarf.

My fangs finally under control, I rose to my feet, noting with chagrin that he stood a good foot taller than me. "You may call me Professor Martin," I said curtly. "And I'll see you in class."

"Your word is my command." He bent to collect his briefcase from where he'd placed it on the floor and then flashed me a toothy grin as he left. I sank into my chair and grabbed for my mug, slurping down the remainder of the contents before rubbing my forehead and sighing deeply.

Class turned out to be relatively uneventful. It usually was. Between 7:00 P.M. and 9:00 P.M., most students typically weren't firing on all cylinders, particularly those holding down full time jobs. I was keenly aware of Peter's presence throughout the class. I tried to avoid looking at him, but couldn't keep ignoring him when he repeatedly raised his hand to answer questions. All of his answers were correct, suggesting he had lied about not doing the reading. I made sure I checked his last name on the class roster before I called on him so I wouldn't lapse back into using his first name. Even when he wasn't participating in the discussion, Peter was watching me. I could feel his eyes boring into me.

Usually, I hung back after class so students could ask me questions, but that night I wanted to get away as fast as I could. I slipped my notes into my satchel and hurried for the door as soon as I'd finished outlining the reading assignments for the next class. Rather than returning to my office, I dashed outside, toward the path that would take me to the dorms.

The night was humid and dark. The only light was provided by the lamp-posts dotted beside the paved pathway. I tried to keep to the shadows, not wanting to startle anyone. The unseasonably warm winter weather had drawn the students outside. They chatted, laughed, and passed joints around, despite the "no drugs on campus" policy. One group of guys gathered around a cooler filled with beer. I could smell it. They were singing something that sounded suspiciously like a sea shanty.

"Hey, Prof! Want a drink?" One of the guys tilted his head and bared his neck at me. I hurried past without making eye contact. "Hey! Elvira! I'm talking to you!"

The boys burst into laughter and cheers as I quickened my pace. I'd seen them around before and knew they were trouble. After a few moments, the sound of that sea shanty – or whatever it was – resumed. Louder than before.

I could sense their blood. Like an ache at the back of my throat. It hadn't been so bad during class because I always made sure to feed before I taught. But now I needed to get back to my apartment in the dorms. With my own private fridge and microwave.

When I dipped my hand into the pocket of my jacket to grab my keycard, I noticed it was shaking. I couldn't get the boy's taunting out of my head. He reminded me so much of another boy. Another campus. Another time. On a night just like this.

I'd been a freshman. Naïve and innocent. Raised in a small town in the Midwest. Not knowing what to expect in a big city university, and flattered by the attention of the cute guy with the scruffy blonde hair and pale skin.

"C'mon, baby," he'd said as he dragged me away from his friends into the shadows. "Don't be such a prude." He'd wrapped his arm around my shoulder and started to grope at my chest, pressing me against the trunk of an oak tree. He popped open the top button of my pink sweater. I'd never worn pink again. Not after that night.

"Say yes, sweetheart. I promise I'll make it good." He rested his forearms on either side of my face against the tree, effectively trapping me, piercing me with bloodshot eyes.

I wanted to move, but I couldn't. Couldn't look away. Could barely control my own breathing.

"Say yes." His voice was a soft command. A chill snaked down my spine. Then I felt myself go limp, as if someone else controlled my limbs.

"Yes." It didn't sound like my voice. But there was no denying that the whispered word came out of my mouth.

"Good girl." His smile exposed him for what he was. By then it was too late.

I'd never remembered anything else about that night. Only what came after. I'd woken in my dorm room with that terrible thirst. I tried to sit up, but hissed at the burning sensation as the sunshine from the window hit my forearm. I realized what I was. And what I'd never be again. I wanted to scream, but no sound came out.

The bastard had turned me. He didn't need to do that. He could have left me to die. Or fed less, and left me alive. Fully human. But he did neither. I swore that if I ever saw him again, I'd make him pay. I looked for him, but never found him. Turned out he wasn't even a student at my campus.

My luck could have been worse. Later that same year, Congress had recognized vampirism as a legal disability under the Americans With Disabilities Act to protect those – like me – prepared to play by the rules. The Democrats had championed the Bill, but had to make a last-minute concession to the Republicans to allow passage of their "tough on vampire-perpetrated crime" Bill. I supported both measures.

Standing outside the front entrance to my building, I flicked the keycard over the lock. My current digs were a far cry from my student housing – more modern design, and I had the benefit of an entire faculty apartment rather than a sad single room. However, the atmosphere was much the same: the scent of sweaty jocks and beer, freshman girls overdoing their cheap perfume, and the omnipresent smell of Ramen Noodles. I didn't remember being able to smell the noodles when I was a student, but my heightened senses now made them much more pungent. They had a papery, salty odor that made my nose twitch.

After entering the main door, I rounded the corner to the hallway that led to my apartment. Unlike the students, I didn't have to share with anyone and I had my very own kitchenette and bathroom. Pretty basic, but it was everything I realistically needed. I light-proofed the bedroom with heavy shades. It was the only place I ever slept during the day. Before I was turned, my father had never let me live in a ground floor apartment. Not safe for a single girl. The ground floor no longer posed a problem for me.

At the last corner before my apartment, I saw them. A bulky red-haired guy in a tight t-shirt that left little to the imagination, and a mousey blonde girl who I recognized as one of my student neighbors. From the looks of it, he was trying to gain access to her room, if not more than that. He gripped her delicate wrist with a meaty hand and whispered in her ear, "C'mon, Shelley. I won't bite." He licked his lips and swallowed. "I'll make it good. Just say yes."

She grinned up at him and fluttered her eyelids, but her hands clenched at her sides.

I strode forward before I could think better of it. "Shelley, is this young man bothering you?"

Her smile fell away as he relaxed his grip on her hand and turned to me, eyes blazing.

"What would you do about it if I was?" he challenged me. "It would be her word against mine."

Shelley shrank back against the closed door to her room.

I planted my hands on my hips, causing the strap of my satchel to slide down my arm and drop to the floor. "I could file a report."

"And you'd be the only witness." He took a menacing step forward. I had to crane my neck up to see his face with its smug self-satisfied expression. "You think that would get you anywhere?" He nodded at Shelley. "Or her?"

I glanced at Shelley. Her eyes were downcast.

"I'd discredit you," the boy continued. "Say you wanted to bite me." He tapped his neck with his index finger causing me to swallow hard. "I'd say you filed the report in retaliation when I refused you. You really want to get fired over this?" He didn't wait for me to answer. Instead, he grabbed Shelley by the elbow and guided her around me. "Let's go to my place. It's vamp-free."

Shelley didn't look at me as she passed, and I didn't do anything to stop them. After all, it wasn't my job to look out for the students. The faculty were only housed in the dorms to informally set an example. That guy could cause a lot of trouble for me if he wanted to. A lot more trouble than I could cause for him.

Shaking my head sadly, I replaced the keycard in my pocket, reached for my satchel and plucked my door key from my pocket. My shoulders slumped as I trudged inside. I didn't bother with the lights. Didn't need them. Inside my domain, all was quiet. I inhaled deeply, relieved by the calming scent of gardenias. I always used a highest strength air freshener to mask the college student scents outside my door. I had never actually slipped before, but I didn't need to be tempted.

I dropped my satchel beside the computer desk and shrugged out of my jacket which I folded over the back of the chair. In the kitchenette, I dumped my keys in the shell-shaped crystal bowl my mother had given me as a house-warming present and then reached for the garish mug, Sarah's gift. I didn't mind using it here. Where no one else would see it.

I fished inside the fridge for a blood-bag, and noticed that my supply was getting low. After switching on the microwave with the bag inside, I ducked into the living area to boot up the ancient desktop computer I'd kept since college as a backup machine. It automatically defaulted to the blood order page and I tapped the code to renew my supply, hitting "enter" just as the microwave beeped.

I poured the blood carefully into the mug and inhaled the coppery goodness. The end of a batch was never as tasty as a fresh order, but it was good enough. Better than the alternative out in the hallway. An image of Peter's grin flashed into my mind and I banished it from my thoughts, taking a big gulp from the mug to steady my nerves. I closed my eyes and forced myself to relax as the warm liquid did its work. The tension eased from my muscles and I felt my canines retract, not even realizing that I had extended them this time.

Heaving a sigh, I took my supper back to the computer desk and set the cup beside the monitor. I sank into the chair and clicked on the icon for my email. While the new messages were loading – which always took a while on this machine – I regarded the framed photograph on the wall. I would have seen it more clearly if I turned the lights on but I could see as much as I needed to in the dark. My parents posed in front of the family home sometime in late spring. Mom's flower beds were in full bloom and dad was squeezing her shoulders, smiling down at her as she mugged for the camera. For me. I remembered taking that shot right after I graduated high school. Dad had told me that my life was just beginning. I could be anything I wanted to be. Do anything I wanted to do. Mom chimed in that she couldn't wait to see what I'd choose to do next.

My gaze darted back to the monitor as the computer dinged, a signal that the messages had finally downloaded. Not much since before my class. Some spam. An ad for new season swimwear as summer was "just around the corner." My heart sank as I deleted it. I used to love spending my summers at the lake near my parents' house, swimming and sunning myself.

There were a few general announcements from the faculty secretary about grading deadlines and student tutoring sessions. And one message from the Dean's Office. The subject line read: *Faculty Meeting*. It was from his executive assistant and contained an audio file – the standard recording of the monthly faculty meeting. Another of my "special accommodations". They couldn't move faculty meetings to the evenings, and I couldn't participate during the daytime, so they agreed to provide me with an audio recording of the debates. I couldn't actually engage in the conversation, but at least I could keep informed.

Absentmindedly, I clicked on the audio icon and leaned back in my chair, sipping from my mug as I listened. The dean was rambling on about budget cuts and classroom renovations for a long time. I was barely concentrating when the discussion turned to faculty hiring.

"We've filled all but one of our open faculty positions over the last three years, but we're still getting slammed on diversity. Our peer institutions continue to do better than us — for reasons of which we're all aware — in raising the ranks of women and minority faculty. Professor Levine will shortly be presenting our hiring report to the Board of Trustees. Seth, do you have anything to share with us about the report?"

The dean's voice was followed by some murmuring and then a cough as Professor Seth Levine cleared his throat and began to speak.

"Not much to add, Dean. We've made six new hires over five departments in the last three years: five Caucasian men, one woman, and one with a recognized disability. So we've only met two of the university's diversity criteria."

Someone else – possibly Professor Dawson – broke in. *"Wait, you said six hires. Isn't that seven hires? Five and two?"*

Professor Levine responded, *"One hire qualified – for want of a better term – in two diversity categories."*

I sat bolt upright and slammed my finger on the mouse button to pause the recording. I knew I was a diversity hire. I probably wouldn't have been interviewed at all otherwise. But to hear my colleagues discussing it in those stark terms – and in my absence – made me feel like a pariah. For heaven's sake, I was as qualified as any other candidate. Ph.D. in history from a top school. On full scholarship. Of course, I wrote my thesis at night, but that probably wasn't so different from a lot of "normal" Ph.D. students. And I contacted my supervisor predominantly via email because of largely incompatible schedules. She had been a self-professed "morning person". But, other than that, my qualifications were the same, if not better, than a lot of other entry-level teaching candidates.

It would never matter how good a teacher or scholar I was. I'd always be that "lady vampire" hired because of my gender and my "disability". I powered down the computer, plunging the room into complete darkness.

Pushing to my feet, I clutched my empty mug to my chest and turned for the kitchen. I was rinsing out the last traces of blood when someone knocked on the door. The sound was light, hesitant. Without my heightened senses, I may not have heard it at all. I plunked my mug into the draining board and went to answer it. I squinted in the light from the hallway. It took a moment to focus on the large hazel eyes looking up at me, framed by a mass of unruly blonde curls. Shelley. Her cheeks were flushed, the blood pumping close to her skin. It would have bothered me if I hadn't just fed.

"Professor? Could I talk to you for a moment?"

"Sure." I took a step back. "Would you like to come in?"

She glanced beyond me, into my private space. "It's kinda dark in there."

"Sorry." I flipped on the light switch, bathing the room in the soft glow of the frosted globe. Other than the computer desk, the sitting area comprised a simple sofa, bookcase and an old cathode ray television set all of which I'd salvaged from my parents' basement before moving into my first apartment when I was a grad student.

"I guess you don't need much light, huh?" Shelley giggled nervously, shifting her weight from one foot to the other.

"Would you rather talk out here?" I gestured to the hallway.

"No, it's fine." She took a deep breath and pushed past me into my living room. "Can I sit down?" She indicated the sofa and I nodded. I shut the door and pulled the desk chair out at an angle for myself so I was sitting close enough to talk without being so close that I might seem threatening.

"What can I do for you?"

"Actually, you already did it. I came to thank you."

"I'm sorry. What did I do?"

"You showed me what a tool Chris is."

"Chris?" I raised an eyebrow.

"Yeah the guy from the –" She nodded at the door instead of completing the sentence.

"Oh, the young man you were with earlier."

"Yeah, that was a big mistake. You showed me I didn't have to stand for it."

"I'm sorry. I'm confused. I thought that you were going to –"

"Yeah, he wanted me to go back to his apartment. I think he wanted to go, like, all the way. And I wasn't ready for that. I mean, I'm not ready for that. I mean, at least not with him." Her voice was breathless. She had her arms wrapped around her waist and her toe tapped against the nondescript industrial carpet.

"And you told him no?"

She nodded quickly, causing her curls to bounce around her shoulders. "I told him no," she repeated with a hint of defiance. "But I don't think I would have drummed up the courage to do it if you hadn't stood up to him first."

"I'm sorry, I really don't think I can take any credit for that."

"No, Professor. Believe me. It was exactly what I needed." She dropped her hands to her sides and clawed the threadbare fabric of the sofa. I really needed to get it re-upholstered. Or replaced.

"I'm so glad I could help, Shelley. I only wish I'd done more."

She didn't respond, but she didn't make any move to leave either. An uncomfortable silence followed. She ran her hands over the edges of the cushions and avoided my eyes.

"Was there something else you wanted to talk about?" I asked, leaning forward slightly, but not too close.

She glanced up at me through thick dark lashes. "Professor, please don't think I'm being rude, but can I ask you something?"

I didn't like where this was going, but she seemed harmless enough. "I suppose."

"You don't have to answer if you don't want to."

"Okay."

"I guess I was wondering why you…" Shelley hesitates as if searching for the right word. "… Backed off when Chris got in your face like that. I mean, you have that thrall power. Couldn't you have made him do whatever you wanted him to do?"

My spine stiffened. "You know that's not allowed, Shelley."

She examined her fingernails carefully as if her strawberry pink polish was the most fascinating thing in the room. "Lots of things aren't allowed on campus, Professor. That doesn't mean people don't do them."

"Well, I certainly don't."

Her hazel eyes opened wide as she glanced up at me. "You mean, like, *never*? You've never actually thralled anyone?" Idly, I wondered if that was a real verb. "But you could, right? I mean, if you wanted to?"

I had no idea what to say. The conversation was straying into uncomfortable territory. The truth was that I had never actually tried to catch anyone in my thrall. After it had happened to me, I couldn't bear the thought of ever doing that to anyone else.

Shelley was twisting her fingers on her lap, and still making no move to leave.

"Did you want something else?" I asked.

Her cheeks flushed and I swallowed hard, trying my best to ensure that my fangs stayed where they were.

"It's just that I had wondered if you purposely didn't, you know, thrall Chris. Like, to teach me a lesson or something."

"What?"

"Well, you forced me to stand up for myself."

A horrified chill slammed into me as if someone had inserted a shard of ice I into my brain. I pressed my fingers to my temples. How could she believe I left her at the mercy of that creep on purpose, when I could have helped? But then, how could she not? That's exactly what I did.

"Professor? Are you okay?" Her voice seemed to be coming from a long way away as the pounding in my head increased. I looked at her through squinted eyes. She was curling back from me, into the far corner of the sofa. "Oh my God!"

Oh no. This couldn't be happening. Not now. Ignoring the girl cowering on my sofa, I darted to the bathroom to check the mirror. That thing about us having no reflection? An old wives' tale. I had discovered that much the morning I turned.

One glance in the mirror showed me all I needed to know. My eyes were bloodshot, the irises rimmed with crimson. Exactly like that guy's had been the night he did this to me. It was a terrible sight, but I couldn't tear my eyes away, turning my face from side to side and pressing my fingertips to my sallow cheeks as I watched in horrified fascination.

I heard the door open and snick shut in the other room. Shelley must have thought I was really going to bite her. I couldn't blame her, even though I'd always been able to control my urges before. I looked back at my reflection – bright red eyes and elongated fangs. The picture of the classic vampire.

As the scent of Shelley's pounding blood dissipated from the apartment, replaced by the sickly faux-gardenia smell I was used to, I forced myself to breathe deeply. The red color gradually leached out of my eyes and the searing pain in my head fell away.

I sank, trembling, to the bathroom floor, tremors running down my arms as I curled them around my shins. I pressed my forehead to my bent knees and tried to hold back the tears that were forming behind my eyelids. I had cried more since I became this ... thing .... than ever before in my life. And I hated the pink tears. Absolutely *hated* them.

I slammed a fist onto the tiled floor in frustration, and heard it crack. What was I supposed to do with all this power and strength? It was so useless. An image of Shelley's panicked face flashed before my eyes, followed by the memory of Peter baring his neck in my office. And of those guys with the beers who had taunted me.

This time I slammed my fist into the floor on purpose. I had all this power and couldn't do anything with it. No, not couldn't. *Wouldn't*. Shelley thought I was trying to teach her. I wasn't, but I could teach some of those idiots who hurt people like her.

But I couldn't do any of that if I didn't learn what I was, and how to use what I had. Sarah's words from last summer played through my mind: *You have to start being what you are.*

I scrambled to my knees and grabbed for the towel on the rail, swiping it across my eyes and glaring at the pink stains my tears had made on it. This was what I was now. I had to own it. I should never have let myself be a victim. Little Shelley was tougher than I was. She stood up to Chris. And what did I do?

I wiped my hands down my face, regarding my reflection in the mirror one last time. Puffy pale cheeks marred by the pink streaks of my tears. I left the stains there and headed for my satchel in the living area. I dug around for my phone and opened my contacts list. Taking a deep breath and letting my fangs elongate of their own accord, I scrolled down until I found the number I was looking for.

Vamps on Campus – Allen University

I hit "call", held my breath, and waited.

Tunnel Vision

Mandy Broughton

"CAN WE KILL THE STENCH?" Peter Sayles squinted, peering through the shadows. He'd already asked for more light and received a negative. Through the thin layer of the Hazmat breathable skin and mask, the odor of the downtown Houston tunnel system remained strong. Rotten cabbages. That's what Peter thought of.

"The aroma of mosquitoes festering in squalid waters and soggy carpet never seeing the light of day," John Sanchez said, mock-breathing in deeply. "Different places. New locations. Same smell."

"This is my perfume." Isabol Kramale clapped her hands. The gloves caused the sound to be muffled. Muted, but loud enough that two men, Rookie and Grunt, picked up the pace. They offloaded the grav carts. Big silver cases splattered with the black gumbo Texas clay so often found on the Coast. Peter didn't know their real names. Isabol called them, and they answered.

Isabol continued, "It's the nature of the beast. It's also why we don't bring top-dwellers to salvage and recovery operations."

Peter grinned in the dark. No one could see it but he was sure they could hear his smile. "Because we complain too much?"

Isabol shrugged. "Most don't find their way back to topside but complaining works too."

Peter laughed but the merriment faded as he realized Isabol was serious. Previous expeditions into this real estate had ended in cave-in fatalities; Peter chided himself for joking around.

Now that flooding had finally cleared and the engineers had made it stable, the trick would be turning the tunnel system into a desirable rental property. If he could take and turn it into leasable retail shops—desirable real estate—he'd turn a profit. And retire with a nice chunk of change, all before turning forty.

But first came clearing. The deluge left broken concrete, rebar and soggy sheetrock in its wake, along with unidentifiable possessions of those surprised by the flood. Debris and reminders of the devastation tended to reduce property values. He'd sweet-talked Isabol into working this operation. Fortunately, she was a risk-taker too—all treasure hunters were. She worked as a salvage expert to finance her treasure hunting ways. And maybe pick up a trinket or two working clean-up along the way.

Dreaming of dollar signs, he asked, "We under the Esperson Buildings?"

Tapping keys on her computer armband, Isabol threw holographic imaging onto the walls. Peter squinted as the red lights crisscrossed and intersected their way throughout the cavern, as the map imaging overlaid onto the crumbling walls. "Travis and

Walker. Yes, the Esperson Buildings," she confirmed. "Where it all started."

Peter was standing close enough to Sanchez to see him frown. "The Hypercane didn't hit here first."

Grunt laughed, a yipping sound that made Peter think of coyotes. "She ain't talking where it hit. She's talking where the tunnels started. Here," he said, pointing downward, "in the 30s."

Sanchez pulled the last case off the cart. "But the Hypercane hit in '49. There wasn't time for all this to be built."

Grunt threw a rock at Sanchez. "Man, you've been underground too long, come up for air. Don't you know history?"

Rookie jumped in, the younger man was eagerness himself. "Not 2030s, sir. The 1930s. Sterling connected two of his buildings with a tunnel. After that, the Esperson Buildings."

Isabol grunted. "Thank you for the history lesson, professor." She tapped her foot, annoyed. A dusty cloud rose from the floor, the dust filtering the light and making a smoky haze appear. "Back to work," she snapped. Rookie jumped to focused attention, the rest of the crew following at a more leisurely pace.

Peter turned a slow circle as Isabol's crew unpacked. Monitoring equipment, spray paint, trackers and other boxes piled high in the room. But room wasn't quite the proper name. With the rubble, cave looked more like it. Cavern wasn't the best name either but humans hadn't been down here officially since before the destruction twenty-five years prior. He eyed a button on the ground. Rubbing his fingers over the plastic, he wondered about the person who'd worn it. The devastation left nothing recognizable save a button or pocketknife.

Sanchez placed remote sensors within the crevices of the broken concrete. "Plenty of people died in the water quakes before the Hypercane hit. I've heard ghosts roam the place, chasing out all who enter."

Rookie glanced side to side, and then lowered his voice. "Mellie Esperson is said to haunt here." He wore the current fashion, brown hair cut in a short Mohawk in back and thick mop in front. Peter wasn't sure how he got it to stay in place under the Hazmat hood.

"All the dearly departed? Saving the tunnel tombs from being disturbed?" Grunt mocked the other two. He looked to be Sanchez's cohort in age but thicker in build than the seasoned cave-diver.

"All I'm saying is why no one's stayed down here too long," Rookie said. "Ghosts."

"Ghost stories," Isabol said. "Children's tales. Besides, Mellie haunts the buildings and the elevators, not the tunnels."

"Elevators used to run to this level," Rookie said. "Before the Hypercane. She could've taken the elevator down here and got stuck."

Isabol harrumphed. Peter thought he heard a mumbled "idiot" as well. Rookie must have heard it or thought better of trying to further justify his position because he quickly looked very busy.

"I don't know about Mellie," Sanchez said. "But ghosts come to chase out treasure hunters. Water quakes caught everyone off guard. Lots of prizes left to be found."

"Because of all the banks down here?" Isabol shook her head slowly, as if she couldn't believe she was in the middle of such idiocy. "Hate to break the news but all the paper money is deteriorated. Water tends to do that to paper."

Peter spied a natural bench covered in flowstone. The striations in the calcite covered the top and sides of the object where water had presumably flowed uninterrupted for twenty-five years, leaving only minerals behind. It reminded him of bridges that boasted quick-forming stalactites found underneath. He sat, fingering the sides. Maybe not so natural.

"There's more than just paper money down here," Sanchez said.

Peter jerked his head up but Sanchez wasn't looking his way. He ran his hand across the smooth stone. "Real estate," Peter insisted. "All that's left is real estate. And I want it cleared." He kicked his legs apart, further spreading out on his chosen perch.

Isabol looked up in the dim light, her pearly whites flashing. "I never assume it's only property I'm clearing."

"For the price I'm paying," Peter said, "let's keep focus on salvaging the property. Treasure hunt on your own time. And dime."

Isabol chuckled.

The rest were silent, save for the clicking and occasional thump of boxes and equipment being unpacked.

"You see any ghosts the last time?" Rookie asked.

"No," Sanchez said. He held a neon green box, a portable seismograph. He attached it to an unbroken piece of sheetrock high over his head. "Only saw men and women down here. Before they became ghosts."

Peter raised an eyebrow but chose not to comment. Instead he studied a shiny rock on the ground. He pocketed it.

"Second air shaft should be straight ahead," Isabol said, ignoring him. "Right in the middle of that mess." Contrary to Peter's intuition, she dimmed the ancient carbide light mounted on her helmet. "Sanchez, take the grunts and open a tunnel to it. I'll take tenderfoot here, and we'll do a preliminary walkthrough."

"Already on it, '*la Jefe*.'" Sanchez clicked the last monitor in place on the broken rebar. "Rookie, take the NW corner and start digging."

Peter heard the gulp through the helmet mic. Sanchez had selected the most precarious of the digging spots for him. Peter smiled, Sanchez had spunk—don't cross him in the future.

"If we're not back in twenty, come after us." Isabol jerked her head at Peter to follow him. She tossed a holographic timer onto the ceiling. A twenty-minute countdown displayed in the middle of the room. Bright red lights ticked off the time, as if a bomb was readying itself to detonate.

Peter was pleased with the work she had done thus far. She knew more about salvaging the underground than many of his engineers. And had a few non-traditional ideas as well—digging new connecting tunnels and solid cementing the tumbled down load-bearing walls instead of clearing. Engineers wanted nice and tidy. Isabol took messy and embraced it. But the attitude could go.

Peter stood. He took one last look at his bench. He could make out four more similar seats embedded in flowstone. Short, maybe three feet in length and two in width with about eighteen inches from the ground. He pocketed another shiny stone.

Rookie and Grunt worked in the farthest end from it. Sanchez barked orders, all three with their backs to Peter. They weren't concerned with his corner. Peter nodded to himself, satisfied. His brief absence shouldn't cause any problems.

"Second air shaft," he repeated. "Then what?"

"That should take the rest of the day," Isabol said. "The rest is up to you, Boss." Her mocking tone made Peter cringe.

They left the room in silence. She'd objected to his joining the clean-up. He had dangled a Queen's ransom before her with the condition that he participated. She capitulated. He was glad he'd made that stipulation. It'd pay off. Peter smiled to himself.

He veered to the left to keep from running into Isabol. Her quick stop brought him out of his daydreaming. They emerged from a stepping stone hallway to another cavern-sized room. She panned her light across the roof and then on the walls. She threw holographic images to overlay broken sheetrock and concrete. "This area is better than the map. Used to be a bank, before the storm."

Peter nodded, then realizing she couldn't see his nod, agreed out loud. "But no paper money to be salvaged."

Peter felt the irritated look versus seeing it. Isabol communicated far more to him than mere words. "I don't go after paper." She tapped the East wall. "The entire East end is a sink hole. And unstable." She pointed to two cave-ins that originally had been off-shoots from the room. "These two tunnels supported the East section."

"Which I don't own and don't care about," Peter said. "I bought best spots to work with. The city's rebuilding and I want to flip this into a gold mine."

"I like gold." Isabol studied the map a second more then flipped it off.

"Gold. Dollar signs. Assets. It's all the same to me." Peter's vision had been gradually improving in the darkness. The red lights of the mapping system hadn't disturbed his night vision.

"You're right about the Southwest section being the least damaged. It's going to take a lot of work to make it stable."

"And I gave your drawings to my engineers," Peter said. "But for now, I only need your expertise on removal. It needs to be desirable. This," he said, indicating the rubble, "isn't."

Isabol agreed.

Peter asked one of several questions that had been on his mind. "Why aren't you afraid? Very few were willing to take this job. You dig through holes smaller than this regularly."

"And more unstable." She gave a full body shiver. "And I volunteered to map one of the deepest recorded sinkholes. Narrowed down like a closed-in well with spikes on the bottom."

"Spikes?"

"Rebar from the crushed concrete. Felt hot down there too. Like descending into hell. But no aquifer."

Peter shuddered himself. A vibration tickled his feet. And it had nothing to do with his apprehension of being underground. The movement lasted a moment before fading off, leaving him to wonder if it really had occurred.

Isabol held up a hand. "Feel that? Another sink hole wanting to open up." She studied her computer. "I have it about a hundred and twenty meters northeast from here. But that tremor makes me think my estimate was wrong. We should be safe enough," she said. Then added, "I hope."

Peter watched her brown eyes survey the hallway. A stray piece of hair circled her mouth. If he hadn't known it was blonde, then he would have guessed it dark from all the shadows and dim lights. He wondered if it bothered her since the Hazmat suit prevented her from pulling it away.

"Why haven't you worked down here before?" he asked.

"Before what?" She marked the two cave-ins with neon green spray paint. For all the advanced technology they had, simple spray paint worked best on marking work.

"Why haven't you cleared the tunnels?" Peter asked.

"Flooding," she replied. Circle with an X through it meant a load-bearing wall. Those were not to be touched, only shored-up and stabilized, if able. She walked down the hallway, marking the debris. Peter wondered if water-diviners had worked their magic a thousand years earlier the same way Isabol divined stable, not-stable, and removable.

"Flooding, my eye," Peter said. "You grew up here. We both remember the headlines as the Hypercane approached. Sanchez is right, there are trinkets to be found. Why travel the world to work underground but not in your own backyard?"

Isabol flashed her pearly whites. "I suppose I didn't have the right incentive until you came along." Her computer beeped. She frowned. "That's odd," she muttered.

"What?" Peter asked. Before Isabol could answer, a low rumbling filled the air. This time Peter didn't feel the floor shake but the room echoed as if a cave-in was occurring. "That's not the sound of a sinkhole forming."

The room filled with a green light and a hazy mist rose up from the floor. The humidity in the chamber was close to ninety percent but the mist looked like it formed from chilled air meeting a warm floor. The ambient air temp in the tunnels had been close to ninety-five degrees.

"What's our temperature?" Peter asked. He rubbed his gloves against his arms.

"Seventy-two and dropping." He heard the confusion in Isabol's voice. They'd descended from the surface in the middle of summer. Houston's heat and humidity were the norm. Even the Gulf waters felt more like a bathtub versus the ocean. And that included the underground. There wasn't a cool spot to be found in the middle of Houston's summer. Unless it was conditioned air and an enclosed space.

"Is there an underwater tube we don't know about? New or otherwise?" Peter watched the mist crawl up the walls. Even through the Hazmat suit, he could now feel the chill. It had to be below sixty degrees. "Do you even know what one sounds like?"

"No," Isabol said. "But if it's a new one forming then we're dead."

The green light outlined Isabol in a shimmering, haze. And their carbide lamps were useless in the fog, like using high beams on a car. But he heard the fear in her voice. And he understood it. Her being afraid was scarier than anything else happening around him.

He'd only been a kid when the Hypercane had hit Houston. Everyone had thought it was only a massive hurricane, a once in a millennial event. No one realized that while still covering the entire Gulf of Mexico, days before landfall, the strength of the storm had sent shockwaves through the shallow shelf to the coastal cities. Those shockwaves dug new canals, filling with saltwater. The Houston tunnel system, decades old and lovingly kept up, didn't stand a chance with the new waves of destruction. The tunnels filled with saltwater. Land became liquefied in an instant. They formed before the people had been fully evacuated. The concrete city couldn't float on the quicksand. Overnight, the land next to the Gulf of Mexico had become a massive Venice, Italy. All without the aid of floatation devices.

"Was this how they felt?" Peter asked. He placed a shaky hand against the sagging gypsum board. "The ones that thought they had time because the Hypercane was still covering the gulf."

"The people? They shut up their businesses for the day and then the salt water tubes opened up," Isabol said. Instinctively, she had moved under an archway, closer to Peter, brushing his arm. She reached out a hand to the feel the wall. "I don't remember how many died in the flooding. Or up above when the bottom fell out from under them. Like Pompeii. They didn't have a clue. Only it was water, not fire this time."

"Over a thousand," Peter said. "One thousand four hundred twenty."

Isabol sucked in a deep breath and held it. She exhaled slowly. "I don't feel any movement," she said. "The deep waters of the Gulf are the only cool spot around here. But I don't feel any movement," she repeated. They stepped lightly on the ground, as if it were too hot to touch.

Or too cold. Cold ocean water could cause the mist. Peter knew if a new channel formed, they were dead. He pushed the thought aside and focused on reason. "The cold air and trembling sound, it's not from beneath us." Peter stopped then started again. "It's not a rumbling anymore. Is it moaning?"

He spun around. From the hallway, a white figure floated through the mist. Peter could see the green light behind the figure, through it. As it drew closer, he began to think of it as a he. Tall—impossibly tall—filling the hall from ceiling to floor and growing larger. Or closer. Peter wasn't sure which. The face contorted in pain, screaming, but only a low moan rumbled through the air.

"That's not a ghost," Isabol said, her voice stumbling over the words.

"Sure," Peter said, not liking the shakiness of his own voice. "So what is it?"

"Jean Lafitte?"

"The dead pirate?" Peter tried to laugh but the apparition shrieked. All noise died on Peter's lips. The scream echoed through the room and bounced off the walls. "BE GONE!"

Peter ducked, pulling Isabol down to the floor with him. He froze. The specter shrieked again. "GONE!" bounced from wall to wall, thundering his eardrums.

He shivered in the coldness of the room. Or maybe it was the ghost's inhuman moaning. His eardrums thudded, like the time he'd taken a seat in front of concert speakers. Boom. Boom. Boom. He couldn't hear anything save the blood pumping through his eardrums.

"It's gone," Isabol whispered. Peter opened his eyes. The green light, ghost, and mist vanished. The chill was gone as well. "And you can get off of me too," she said, pushing on his chest. Peter rolled to the side and lay stretched out catching his breath. Isabol jumped to her feet and held out a hand to him.

"Thanks for the tackle and save," she said, "but next time maybe you shouldn't eat such a big lunch."

"And I'll have them hold the mushrooms." Peter brushed the dust off his Hazmat suit. "Those were hallucinations, right?"

Isabol grunted. "I have playback on my band." Peter watched over her shoulder. A shaky hand thumbed through the computer. Playback. The tiny screen strapped to her right arm leapt to life. The vitals of the entire salvage party scrolled down the left side of the screen. Blood pressure, heart rate and breathing spiked for him and Isabol while the men in the other chamber ran normal. Sanchez was almost below normal metrics.

"What the—," Peter mumbled as the screen turned to snow. Nothing showed on the screen, not even the mist or green light. "What happened?"

"EM pulse," she said. Peter was close enough he could see her lick her lips. "We got hit with an EM pulse."

"An electro-magnetic pulse?" Peter asked. "Conveniently wiping out all our recordings and computer work?"

"I'm not sure how convenient it is." Isabol tapped again. Screen still showed snow. "But that's what it looks like when it hits." She touched the carbide light on her helmet. "That's why we try to use non-electronic tech down here as much as possible.

Peter pointed with a blue-gloved finger. "You expected to get hit with an EM pulse? Or is that just when meeting new ghosts?"

"No ghosts. But the moisture in the air makes the electronics wonky." Isabol chewed her lip and then swiped the computer off. "I'm going to find out what they did. What did they release into the underground? And it wasn't Mellie Esperson," she muttered. She marched to the previous chamber.

"Sanchez! I want to talk to you—" Isabol's rant was cut short. "Peter, come help me."

She dashed ahead. Peter couldn't see anything except Isabol's light bouncing as she ran and then it dropped.

Peter's heart fell. It was a sinkhole after all. Or a salt tube. Unrecorded gases affected their reasoning and the computers must have glitched. Isabol was probably dead, falling into a sinkhole, chasing after Sanchez. Sanchez had fallen after the other two men. Now Peter would spend the rest of eternity with Jean Lafitte's ghost—

"Peter, help me," Isabol called again. This time Peter ran. But then stopped. The carbide light cast a low light ahead. Blackness against a dark floor. The shadows played tricks, each step he expected not to find purchase but emptiness. Hole. Salt tube. Anything but terra firma.

Shuffling his feet forward, he rounded the corner and saw why her voice sounded so frantic. Isabol crouched over a man, Sanchez, from the looks of his pants. She ran her med computer over his chest.

"Med eval?" Peter crouched beside her. Sanchez lay motionless. In the gloom, he couldn't tell if the man was pale or not.

Isabol thumped her computer in frustration. "It's not working." She leaned back, sitting on her heels. "I don't know—"

Sanchez grunted and then a long snore escaped from his lips.

"He's asleep," Peter said.

She rubbed her forehead. "Asleep?"

Peter grabbed the man's hand and took a pulse. Strong, even through the thin Hazmat layer. Once Peter was close in, he could see the steady rising and falling of the man's chest. And another snore came over the mic. "Surely not a second time," Peter said.

"What?"

Peter ignored her question. "Gases. Has he been exposed to something that would cause this? Maybe we're next."

Isabol shook her head. She tapped her Hazmat suit's bright yellow tag close to her left shoulder. "The canaries would pick up any change in air filtration or failure immediately, even non-lethal. They aren't electronic. They're chemical." A slow flush rose in her cheeks. It was dark enough, he could see the change even in the shadows.

Peter frowned. He brought a hand to his chin but wasn't able to rub it because of the suit. He settled for fingering the yellow air filtration tag, lovingly referred to as a canary. He wondered about the miners of old, had they minded bringing live songbirds to the underground? Knowing that any released gases would kill the canaries first.

"So what do we do now?"

Isabol whacked Sanchez on the head. "Wake up, Sleeping Beauty. Your prince has arrived. Your prince of doom. Your prince of all bosses. Your prince of 'I'll fire your—'"

Peter thumbed down the volume in the headsets. He stood and inspected the chamber around him as the tirade continued. This wasted time. Where were the other men?

When Isabol took a breath, Peter touched her shoulder. "If Sanchez is asleep, where are the other two? Shouldn't they be worried about him?"

Isabol grunted, standing. "Probably taking an extra long sleep break themselves. All on my dime"

"Which is ultimately my dime. Our twenty minutes is long gone. Why is Sanchez alone in the outer chamber?"

Sanchez rubbed his legs, as if trying to regain circulation. "Boss," he told Peter, "I promise I wasn't sleeping—"

Isabol shoved her arm band computer into his face, showing him the readings. The readings showed snow so she hissed, "snoring," instead.

Sanchez stumbled but continued. "I wasn't sleeping. It was a ruse. The two new men you hired, they're up to something." He rubbed his arms as if to warm them. Or wake them up.

"I guess I accidentally fell asleep watching them."

"Idiot."

Peter shifted his weight on his feet. "Listen, I hate to disturb the company meeting and all but I want to check on the others."

Isabol stopped talking. She frowned, her eyebrows forming a deep "V". She marched into the other chamber with Sanchez meekly following. He looked behind at Peter and shrugged his shoulders occasionally. As they approached, even without the help of the mics, Peter could hear metal hitting stone and concrete. Peter relaxed, slightly.

The main entrance chamber wasn't any different from when they had left. But Peter felt like he was a different person. He'd seen Jean Lafitte's ghost—for a lack of a better description—and now walked into a chamber where two workers were busily clearing the tunnel branching to the Northwest.

Peter sat on his bench, opposite from them, this time relaxing completely.

Isabol plants both fists on her hips. "You two are looking extraordinarily busy."

Rookie tried the wide-eyed innocent look and failed. Grunt grinned.

"Care to explain about Sanchez?" Isabol asked.

Grunt stopped shoveling the rocks and broken concrete. "Sanchez fell asleep leaning against the wall. It was the one marked to clear. We tried to wake him. When he didn't, we carried him to the outer chamber to be out of our way. You and the financier," Grunt jerked his head to Peter and gave him a leering grin, "took so long that we thought it'd be best to just keep working."

Red digital countdown flashed -00:08:57. Isabol chewed her lip. Peter figured she was about to light into them again but was surprised when she was silent. He found another shiny rock and picked it up. Everyone stood as if in a five-way standoff.

"What'd you boys find?" Peter tossed the rock and plucked it out of the air. He kicked his long, lean legs in front of him, crossing them at the ankles.

"Nothing," Grunt said.

"That true, Rookie? You find nothing?" Peter pocked the rock. "Because we found something."

"Treasure?" Sanchez asked.

"Better," Peter said.

"A lot of treasure," Sanchez breathed. Peter chuckled. Isabol crossed her arms and stood out of sight.

"Not possible," Grunt muttered.

Rookie cocked his head to the side. "You didn't find any treasure. You only found a—"

"Yes?" Peter stood. "We only found what?"

"A ghost," Rookie finished lamely.

Grunt punched the kid. He hit him hard enough in the gut that Rookie doubled over.

"Hey," Peter said, positioning himself between the two men. He laid a gloved hand close to Grunt's chest but refrained from touching him. Anger flashed through Grunt's eyes. Peter could see that in the dim light, clearly. Anger and something else. Greed?

"You found something, didn't you?" Peter put the pieces together. The ghost. The EM pulse. "Where? In the second air shaft?" He smiled, not a warm welcoming smile of a friend and chum. But a cold-calculating smile of predator ready to pounce. Many business foes had seen that smile before their financial demise.

"Second air shaft isn't done," Isabol said.

"It is. They just filled it back up." Peter licked his lips. He could taste the future. It was bright. And full of dollar signs.

"What do you mean, it's already filled it back up?" Isabol demanded. She inspected her armband. She ripped the useless computer off and flung it against the rock pile. She conducted a visual.

"What are you, stupid?" She demanded of the two. "Rule number one in any underground operation, cut the second air shaft in case of a cave-in. Don't fill it back in."

Sanchez sucked in a breath. Isabol looked at him and then Grunt and Rookie. Peter could almost hear the wheels clicking into place. "You were going to cause a cave-in and leave us down here to die."

"Not necessarily," Rookie said. "Uncle said if we could scare you off then we wouldn't have to kill you."

This time Grunt connected with Rookie's jaw. This dropped Rookie to his rear. "You talk too much."

"Scare us off?" Isabol rounded on Grunt. "Is that what the ghost was about?"

"What ghost?" Sanchez asked.

Peter answered, "Isabol and me took longer because we came across the ghost of Jean Lafitte."

"He's the new Cajun operation in town, isn't he?" Sanchez asked. "Trying to horn in on our business? These two jokers sign up with him to double-cross us?"

"Jean Lafitte is the pirate who lived in Galveston in the 1700s," Peter said. "That was a stroke of brilliance. I do appreciate the effort to scare of off before trying to kill us."

Grunt snorted. "It's because my partner died in the last cave-in, I had to take my sister's son into the family business. But he has no taste for killing. Wanted to be in the movies."

"You rigged the ghost?" Isabol asked.

Rookie smiled, still sitting on his butt. "Did you like it? I love special effects. It's so hot and humid down here that I wasn't sure the conditioned air would work, even for a short burst. But I was able to drop the temp enough to touch the high 50s. And the ghost, I thought of him more of one of the Allen brothers, not Jean Lafitte. But then I realized Mellie Esperson was supposed to haunt the buildings above us, so I tried to plant the idea about her haunting the place." Rookie shrugged. "He's a simple holographic projection. I knew the visual wouldn't work on you but maybe the visual with the temperature drop would. And the moaning. Sound is always the killer."

Peter fingered the stones in his suit's pockets. "And the EM pulse?"

Rookie tapped the ground with his hand, jiggling the pebbles and dislodging them. "I hate to down a perfectly good system but there wasn't any way to fake it on-camera."

"I don't understand," Isabol said. "Why scare us off?"

"For the same reason you wanted to salvage the tunnel system here but not before twenty-five years have passed." Peter pulled a rock and tossed it in the air.

Isabol grinned and then laughed. "All right, I get that. So we're all down here for the same thing, a treasure hunt. Wait twenty-five years, and rights revert to the finder. Poor Sanchez. He's the dumb schmuck that has no idea what's going on."

"No, Isabol, you misunderstood him," Peter said. "And underestimated him. But I didn't. Sanchez knows what's going on because I hired him to watch my back."

Isabol narrowed her eyes, glaring at Peter. "He works for me."

"Let's say he works for both of us. As soon as I decided I wanted to revitalize the Houston tunnel system, I wanted the last man known to traverse it. The last one alive."

Isabol whirled on Sanchez. "Does he know how you survived?"

Sanchez smiled. "Yes. He knew I survived by falling asleep in an outer chamber. He didn't hold it against me. Mr. Peter suspected everyone would try to double-cross him. He wanted someone to cover his back."

Isabol smacked her helmet. "I may be harsh but that's how we survive in the in underground." She sat. "But what I don't get, is that no one has found the treasure yet. Isn't this all premature?"

"No," Peter said. "These two jokers have found it. Some of it, at least. They're trying to keep it for themselves." He tossed the two glittery stones to Isabol.

She inspected them. "Where?"

Peter stood at the second air shaft. He grabbed a shovel. Grunt moved as if to stop him but Sanchez and Isabol blocked his way. Peter dug the shovel into the pile. Debris spilled out. Broken concrete. Rebar. Metal. And more shiny rocks. "Bingo."

"You found the jewels?" Isabol dug through the rubble with her gloved hands. "And left them mixed in with the broken concrete?"

Neither Grunt or Rookie said anything. Peter kept an eye on them. "Best hiding place is out in the open. I don't know if they found the rocks in the preliminary blasting or during the cut to the second air shaft—" Peter paused and looked at Rookie.

"Prelim," Rookie said. "Dumb luck."

Sanchez laughed. "Best kind."

"They found the rocks immediately which sped up the entire timetable." He wanted to continue but Grunt had made a move. Peter leapt out of the way when Grunt raised his arm. Peter expected a flash or a deafening boom. What he didn't expect was for Grunt to seize and crash board-like to the ground.

Isabol held up her hand. A Taser. "I keep it for the big rats we find." She looked at Grunt and pulled the gun from his hand. "Sometimes they turn out to be human." She dropped to her knees and brushed her hands over the loose gems. Rubies. Diamonds. Emeralds. Some were as large as her fist and each worth a year's salary, others twice that. "Now what?"

"I suppose you all get a small finder's fee," Peter said.

"No," Isabol said. "We split it, evenly."

"I'm the owner—"

"Salvage workers split all found treasure equally," Sanchez said.

Peter eyed the man. "So you are double crossing me?"

"No, sir," Sanchez said. "Just looking out for everyone, myself included. Law says after twenty-five years, finders keepers. Even I know that." He nodded to Isabol. "She'd agree. *'La Jefe'* splits all treasures with the workers. Always have."

"Always will." Isabol laughed again.

"Even with those two bozos?" Peter jerked a thumb to the still-seated Rookie. Grunt had turned himself over, the Taser wearing off. He breathed heavily.

"All workers." Isabol crossed her arms. "Read the contract."

"Which is why you didn't want me down here to begin with." Peter sighed. He sat on his perch, as if defeated.

"Don't worry," she said. "We'll make sure you get your one fifth share." Isabol laughed. She dumped the contents of an equipment case. She filled it with the precious cargo.

"It was only one cart of precious stones stolen from the vault before the Hypercane," Sanchez said. "Too bad it wasn't all of them."

"Six carts of jewels and precious stones were taken out of the vault at the Houston Museum of Natural Science. The rumor was that only one cart was diverted down to the underground to escape but got caught in the water quakes." Peter told the room. No one appeared to be listening.

Rookie joined the other two in gathering gems. The crate filled up quickly.

Sanchez tossed crumbled sheetrock to the side. "When this wall collapsed, it broke the container open, spilling the contents?"

"That's what we figured," Rookie said. "Or the blast. Either way, we're rich." *Thunk.* Another rock in the box.

Peter leaned back. "The museum knew a heist was in the planning. The thieves planned to burgle the jewels aboveground during the evacuation confusion."

Grunt pushed himself onto all fours. "We know our history. We lived it, even though we were kids. That is, except my nephew."

"A heist. Diverted treasure. At least we found one," Isabol said. "It looks like this contained only loose stones, no jewelry. Too bad."

"What if we pooled the treasure and put it on display?" Peter asked. "We could make a lot of money with it touring the world. 'Pre-

Hypercane relics.' I'd be willing to split all proceeds five ways."

Isabol rubbed her chin. Sanchez looked at her. "No, thanks," both of them said together.

Peter shook his head as he watched the four adults crawl around on the cavern floor looking for jewels. He refused to move his feet when they came close to his bench. He sat there, watching them act like the fools they were.

Isabol took charge of divvying up the loot. Each man greedily held out his hands, pocketing the treasure. Isabol left a neat pile of rocks, Peter's share. He grunted.

When the work was done, Isabol stood. Equipment tossed to the side as the looters held their trinkets in the clay covered hard back cases.

"Those are mine," Peter said. "I paid for all the equipment down here."

Isabol pulled a very large and yellow diamond from her stash and tossed it to Peter's pile. "This will cover the cost of the hardbacks. And I suppose you'll understand why we can't finish the job…"

Peter nodded. Grunt and Rookie hurried out of the cavern, ascending the steps to the surface painstakingly cut and paid for with Peter's money. They never looked back.

Sanchez stood at the base of the stairway. "Thanks, Boss," he said to Peter. "I'm glad you gave me a chance."

Peter waved him off. "I'm glad you could watch out for yourself."

Sanchez ducked his head and followed the other two to the surface.

"My offer stands," Peter told Isabol when they were alone. She stood like a statue, not moving. "We could join together and put the gems on display. Tour the world."

"Thanks, but no thanks," Isabol said. She moved forward, stiffly at first then loosening up. "In another life, I could have done it but not now. This," she said, pointing to the loaded grav cart. "This will help me retire."

"It's not enough to retire," Peter said. "Just a small drop in the bucket. There's more—"

"It's enough for me to start. And, maybe, one or two more hits and I'll be set. Mexico City dug a new canal finding another lost city. I think it'll pay off working salvage there," Isabol said. She pushed forward, taking two steps before stopping. "I'm sorry."

"Me, too," Peter said sadly as he watched her ascend to the surface. He sat on his bench for a solid twenty minutes before moving. The timer, which no one had reset, read -00:52:14 and continued counting backwards.

Peter panned his light around the entire cavern. Spray paint cans. Portable seismographs. Shovels. A sledgehammer. "I'm sorry I'll have to find a new crew to haul this out of here."

Reluctantly, he stood. He looked at his perch. Such a nice resting place during the entire ordeal. He grabbed a sledgehammer and he swung it to his bench. *Thunk.* He swung again. *Thunk-thunk.* Calcite broke. *Thunk-thunk-thunk.* He swung harder. Fragments flew. Peter howled at the release of frustration. *Thunk. Thunk. Thunk-thunk-thunk.* The flowstone chipped away eventually revealing a black box.

Peter smiled. He dropped the hammer. A trickle of sweat ran down Peter's forehead but he couldn't wipe it off. No matter, it felt good. He dropped to a crouch and inspected the lock. Broken. Most likely during one of his swings.

He tried to lift the top. Age and disuse held the lid tight but after a few muscled attempts, the lid swung open. A silver tiara with emeralds inlaid sat on top of a velvet cloth. Peter pushed the cloth to the side. Underneath, a garnet ring sparkled in Peter's carbide light. He tried the ring on a gloved pinky. It fit but the stone was three inches in diameter. Whoever wore that ring didn't do much work with their hands.

He removed the ring and continued to dig through the box. Necklaces, uncut gems, another tiara, all lovingly packed for transit.

"They thought they knew their history," Peter told an amethyst necklace. The thing felt like it weighed four pounds. He held it to his neck. "But they didn't dig deep enough. All six cases were evacuated through the underground. Not just one. They weren't stolen. They were lost." He laid the necklace next to the tiara. He patted it, as if to say it was in safe hands now.

He looked beyond his treasure chest to the four other stone seats, all similarly shaped as his perch had been. He grinned. "Mother's Day is coming up. I think shopping in the tunnels will work out nicely."

He grabbed the sledgehammer again and worked to free the other lost jewels.

Thank your for purchasing

Space City 6

If you enjoyed it, please consider leaving a review on your favorite book-sharing site.

Please visit us at

http://spacecityscribes.wordpress.com/

Bios

Artemis Greenleaf has always been fascinated by the mysterious, and she devoured fairy tales, folk tales and ghost stories since before she could read. In 1995, she had a near-death experience which turned her perception of the world upside down. She lived to tell the tale (and often does, in one form or another). Artemis lives in the suburban wilds of Houston, Texas with her husband, two children and assorted pets. She writes novels, short stories, and non-fiction, and her work has appeared in magazines. Upcoming novels include a stand-alone YA called *Exit Point*; and *Dragon Killer* and *The Devil's Advocate,* both of which belong to the Marti Keller Mysteries series. For more information, please visit artemisgreenleaf.com.

Ellen Leventhal is a local author and educator. Ellen has a BA in Elementary Education and an M.Ed. in Special Education. She began her career as a special education teacher and continued as a classroom teacher, working with both elementary and middle school children. Each summer, Ellen teaches creative writing in the WITS/ Rice School

Literacy and Culture Program's Creative Writing Camp. Ellen's writer's dream came true when her first children's book, written with Ellen Rothberg, was published in 2006. The book, *Don't Eat the Bluebonnts,* was the beginning of the South Pasture Series. *Hayfest, A Holiday Quest* and *Bully in the Barnyard* soon followed. Currently, she is busy working on a middle grade chapter book, other picture books, and a compilation of children's poetry.

Monica Shaughnessy draws on her experience as a lifelong Texan by creating characters larger than the Lone Star State. Her work spans multiple genres, including adult mystery and suspense, YA, middle grade, and young reader, but everything carries her signature offbeat style. Her upcoming releases include *The Black Cats, Book Two in the Cattarina Mystery Series,* and *Space City 6,* an anthology of Houston-based stories. When she's not slaying adverbs and polishing her own work, she's helping other writers craft their stories through her developmental editing business. To learn about her books and her editing, visit her online at www.monicashaughnessy.com.

Ellen Rothberg wrote and illustrated her first children's book with a friend at the age of 7, and although she no longer draws the pictures, she still likes to write with a friend, Ellen Leventhal. She is a former elementary school teacher and currently serves as a school counselor. She loves writing with children and helping them express their ideas and feelings. The idea for *Don't Eat the Bluebonnets* was hatched during a visit to her daughter at Texas A & M University. She wondered out loud about the cows eating the bluebonnets, and in the best tradition of that old Texas legend, thought it might be against the law for cows to eat them. Whatever the future holds, she knows it will include creative writing and working with children.

Kaleigh Castle Maguire is a wife and mother of three who loves fiction writing and reading fiction of all genres. She has a particular passion for young adult and children's books and is currently working on two young adult novels - one is a science fiction story for girls and the other is a fantasy action adventure for boys. She is a member of RWA, AWP and SCBWI. She loves to blog about books, writing, and to interview new authors when she can get them to agree (which they happily do most of the time). She's also a proud member of the Houston-based Space City Scribes author collective. In July of 2014, she joined the blogging team at Luna Station Quarterly, contributing interviews with women speculative fictions authors.

Mandy Broughton cannot resist the irresistible force of reading and writing science-fiction. In Fall, 2014, she has two sci-fi short stories being published in the Houston Writers Guild's *Tides of Possibilities* science-fiction anthology. She also has a trio of middle-grade mysteries and one includes a flying saucer! Her adult cozy, *The Cat's Last Meow*, does not have a flying saucer but does have a cat, which is almost as good. And looking farther to that publishing horizon, she has two novels coming in late 2014. One is a historical horror ("run, Quincey, run!") and another cozy, *Sliding into Murder* ("batter-up, oops, she's dead"). Visit her online at www.MandyBroughton.com or on twitter @MandyBroughton. She will talk to anyone who will listen in 140 characters or less.